SARAH BIGLOW

MOLLY ZENK

USA TODAY BESTSELLING AUTHORS

SPECTRAL
A Cayelle Imprint

Hunted Book 3

For permission requests, contact the publisher below:
Cayélle Publishing/Spectral Imprint
Lancaster, California USA
www.CayellePublishing.com

Orders by U.S. trade bookstores and wholesalers, please contact Freadom Distribution:
Freadom@Cayelle.com

Categories: 1. Fantasy 2. Vampires 3. Romance
Printed in the United States of America

Cover Art by Ljiljana Romanovic
Interior Design & Typesetting by Ampersand Book Interiors
Edited by Dr. Mekhala Spencer

ISBN: 978-1-952404-62-7 [paperback]
ISBN: 978-1-952404-61-0 [ebook]

Library of Congress Control Number 2021932845

CHAPTER ONE

EDITH

THREE MONTHS LATER

"TALK TO ME, RED LEADER. WHAT DO YOU SEE?" Dan's voice crackled over our Bluetooth communication links, as we slunk in the near pitch darkness, through what was known as the graveyard, but was, in actuality, the holding stop for the vampire's supply trucks. It still felt strange being on the opposing side to my vampire brethren, but they started this war, not us. I could not blindly follow Mr. Heart song anymore—war or no war.

"Why do we have to be a boring color like red?" Hope complained to the air, and by default Dan, who was safely back at the vampire base

"Why can't we be something fun like pink or glitter?"

"Glitter isn't a color, stupid," her sister, Angel, hissed from my left.

"I'm not stupid, you're stupid," said Hope. She tried to reach around me to punch her sister in the arm, but I held her back.

"That's enough," I warned. "We don't need a mini sibling war in the middle of a real civil war. If you two can't behave, you'll stay behind on the next mission."

"Sorry, Mama E," the girls chorused.

"Still waiting for an answer here," Dan's voice reminded me. I wasn't quite sure how I got stuck being Red Leader, but as the only adult vampire on the Hunters' side, they expected me to take up some leadership role. I knew the clan's methods and movements. I was an asset … or so the Hunters kept telling me. I suspected their real motive was to make sure I didn't defect to the other side.

"We see four supply trucks," I told Dan. "Perhaps a fifth, but it is smaller. Less of a cargo van and more of a pickup truck. What do you see on the radar? Has the clan figured out we're here yet?"

"Not yet, but it's only a matter of time," Dan said. "They always seem to know we're coming."

"That's because someone is still tipping them off," Darren's voice said over the comm link. We had split up to run the mission and gone into different entrances. I had Hope and Angel with me, and he had Parker. "Maybe you should have stayed back at the base to keep an eye on your boyfriend, Angel."

"Caden isn't compromised anymore," Angel said. "And, even if he was, he wouldn't remember if he was tipping off Mr. Heartsong or not."

"That's why he's still dangerous," Darren said.

"Stick to the mission," Dan warned. "How are you doing, Parker?"

"Is giving a shout out to your boyfriend what you call sticking to the mission?" Darren grumbled. "Real mature, Danny. We're counting on you to keep us safe and you're playing verbal footsie with—"

"Only problem I see with the mission is we have four supply trucks and only two people who can drive," Parker said, ignoring Darren's griping. "And no keys. I doubt Heartsong or his lackeys would leave the keys in the ignition waiting for someone to steal their food and weapons."

"Leave that to us," said Hope. She grabbed Angel's hand, and they zipped towards the trucks with the aid of their vampire speed. "Door's open! Awesome!"

"Be careful!" Darren said. "It could be a trap."

"Everything could be a trap," Angel scoffed. "Well, guess what, Darren? We're still alive."

"But you're not invincible, girls," I reminded them. "No one is."

"Maybe not, but we can be useful." Hope fiddled with something near the truck's steering wheel before the engine sprang to life. They high fived each other before clamoring down the line of trucks, repeating the process as they went.

"Okay, you'll never hear me admit this again, but that's some seriously impressive shit, girls," Darren said. "Where did you learn to hot-wire cars?"

"Cambodia. 1972," Angel said. "We can sort of drive too, as long as it's in a straight line."

"Four trucks, four drivers. Great job." Parker said as he and Darren joined me near the trucks. They each picked a truck. I climbed in next to Hope. I hated leaving Angel or anyone alone, but Hope would be the most likely to get distracted and crash if it came to a chase. Even with Dan's real-time surveillance from the base, I still had my doubts on us getting out of there unnoticed.

"We told you we could be useful, Mama E!" Hope settled into the driver's seat, her feet barely reaching the pedals.

"I always knew you were useful, *Bopha*," I said. "Darren is the one who needs convincing."

"Well, this should help, right?" She may be a fifty-five-year-old vampire but Hope still had the innocence and the need to please traits of a child.

"Absolutely, *Bopha*." I smiled. "I'm proud of you and your sister."

"We got incoming!" Dan called over the comm link. "Heat sensor shows—shit—fifteen vamps in the graveyard—with ten more where they came from. Get out of there while you can!"

Darren threw his truck door open and jumped down. I saw the glint of weapons already in his hands before his feet even hit the ground. He wasn't planning to face off with the vampires on his own, was he?

"Parker. Girls. Get out of here, even if you have to run some of 'em over," he said. "I'll hold them off and try to give you as much time as I can."

"Not without me, you aren't." My feet were on the ground before anyone—least of all Darren—could object. "You heard him, girls. I'm counting on you, Parker, to lead the way back to the base. Now go!"

Parker peeled out of there faster than I thought possible for a cumbersome supply truck. He took out a locked fence gate in his bid to find the straightest path to safety, followed closely by Angel and Hope in their own hot-wired trucks.

Once we were alone with the incoming vampire horde, Darren looked over at me and grinned. "You ready for a fight?"

I clutched my fountain pen. It was the only *weapon* I felt comfortable wielding against my vampire brethren. "Only if you are."

He shifted to a fighting stance. "I'm always ready."

"Twenty-five against two is not exactly a fair fight." Despite being outnumbered, I felt fairly calm and capable with Darren beside me. At times, it felt like we could take on anything together.

"Odds bore me." He pivoted and landed a sharp stab to the heart of the nearest vampire. "I like results. Let's do this."

I took a breath and followed him into the fray.

CHAPTER TWO

DARREN

NO MATTER HOW MANY VAMPIRES I'VE DUSTED in the last decade, I still get this rush every time the first one turns to dust under my hand. Tonight was no different. Months ago, if it was well past two in the morning, it would have meant I was tired and sluggish. But, the day Heartsong declared war on humanity, we went into survival mode. That meant teaming up with other bases across the country for coordinated efforts, and sleeping during the day to eliminate the vampire's advantage.

"Behind you!" Edith called as she slammed her fist into an oncoming vamp's throat. It hissed a garbled sound at her before she pressed the point of the pen and slammed it straight into his chest.

"Two down, twenty-three to go!" I called and ducked out of range of two oncoming bloodsuckers.

"I am aware of the math," she called back to me, as a vamp with foaming lips jumped on her back.

Once upon a time, she would have probably yelped out of surprise. Tonight, she just grabbed the asshole around the neck and flung him over her head, making him collide with his buddies like a bowling pin. I slammed my knives into more undead hearts, mentally counting them as they fell; some turning to dust and ash, while others were too new to their afterlives to crumble. They just fell across each other, their gazes unblinking as the remains of their blue blood pooled on the ground.

"Seventeen!" I shouted to Edith as I continued to wade through bodies.

"Must you keep score? It is so distasteful," she gestured to the last supply truck.

I hopped behind the wheel and revved the engine. "You're just mad because I beat you."

Danny's voice came over the comm link. "If you two are done doing your weird flirty thing, can you confirm you're on your way back?"

"On the road now, baby brother," I answered and followed the path Parker had run, the tires trundling over the uneven terrain created by the downed fence.

I couldn't help flipping off the place as we sped away. It hadn't gone perfectly by any means, but we'd all come out of it intact and breathing. That was about as much as we could ask for from this mission.

"Did the girls and Parker make it back to base?" Edith asked as I zipped down back roads, taking an alternative route just in case we'd picked up a tail.

"Just got back," Danny replied.

I watched Edith's posture relax as soon as his words came over the comm link. I understood her worry about their safety, but even I had to admit the girls had come a long way in the last three months. They'd been devoting their time to training.

"Did you know they could hot-wire cars?" I probed as I pulled down a side alley that would lead us to the base.

"I'd forgotten they had such skills before they came into my life," she murmured, her gaze going unfocused for a minute. "We wouldn't have had such success without them."

"I'm not arguing that. Just, maybe next time they should tell us about any other hidden talents that might be useful in a pinch."

"I'm sure they'll be happy to oblige."

The conversation died down as we made the last turn, the base coming up in front of us. I pulled down the street and into a covered garage where two mechanics were already busy stripping the vehicles for parts while another pair of Hunters were inventorying the stolen supplies.

I killed the engine before climbing out and heading to the street, Edith, hot on my heels. I shuddered to think what the police thought was going on here. They probably thought we were an illegal chop shop, but at least they hadn't come knocking down our doors, poking their noses around yet.

"I'm gonna to check in with Harrison. I'll see you up there in a while," I told Edith and gave her hand a squeeze before heading towards the main office.

"Sounds like a success, Paxton," Harrison said, not looking up from his computer when I walked in.

"More than we expected but nothing we couldn't handle," I answered, standing at attention even if he wasn't looking at me.

"Good. Well, get some rest."

"Yes, sir." I pivoted half a step before turning back. "I think he's recruiting again. Far more of the ones I took out tonight didn't turn to dust."

That got his attention. "Dirty bastard."

I'd say Heartsong was forcing people to be turned into vampires, but that wasn't how it worked. No consent meant any potential new recruit would just die from the bite and blood loss. But something told me he wasn't above using a little mind fuck to get them to agree to his terms.

I headed down the hall to Ops, expecting to find Danny still there, shepherding more missions from the safety of the base, but his chair was empty, his headset slung over the back of it.

"He's downstairs," Sam said from the doorway behind me.

I turned to look at her. We'd buried the hatchet months ago and were actually on decent speaking terms. She'd also taken it upon herself to guide Danny through his recovery and rehab.

"He's not supposed to be down there," I growled.

"Stubbornness is a family trait," she quipped as I pushed past her and bolted down to the training room.

Danny leaned against one of the training dummies, sweat shining on his face as he tried to maneuver without his knee brace.

"What the fuck are you doing?" I yelled, resisting the urge to tackle him to the floor. Doing that would only make his injury worse.

"It's been three months," he huffed, sliding down to the ground, his leg outstretched in front of him.

"And the doctor said you'd be lucky to get full mobility back in a year, dipshit."

"It's been feeling better," he said, his lower lip quivering, and I knew he was holding back tears from the pain.

I grabbed the brace from the floor and wrapped his knee back up, securing it tight. He winced, but I didn't care. I refused to let him hurt himself. "You're lucky Sam wasn't with me or she'd have kicked your ass."

"I'm supposed to be a Hunter, D, not some voice in your ear."

I wrapped him in a hug. "You were the kid who hated all of this just a few months ago, remember? You just wanted to hang with your vampire friends."

"Being nearly killed changes your priorities, and Caden is my friend. I should have been able to stop him."

"No. No feeling guilty about this. He caught you off guard and he took advantage of that."

"I just want to be useful again," he sighed.

"You were great tonight," I said, but he shook his head, tears sparkling in his eyes.

"It's not the same. You guys go out risking your lives and I'm stuck here."

If I could keep him here indefinitely, I would, if it meant he'd be out of the line of fire. I couldn't stomach losing him for good. But I knew he'd hate me for saying that. He'd think I viewed him as weak. So, I said nothing and just hauled him back to his feet and guided him to the stairs, waiting, as he hobbled up the flight. At least he could manage that without getting out of breath these days.

"Go get some rest, Danny," I said and patted his shoulder before heading to the dorms myself. I had a girlfriend to decompress with. As I took the turn towards the bedroom, I marveled that, I, in fact, had a girlfriend. Wonders never cease.

CHAPTER THREE

EDITH

I CHANGED INTO MY SILKY NIGHTGOWN AND BEGAN my nightly ritual of brushing my hair for one hundred strokes. It was an old habit my mother insisted on and, at least in my case, old habits definitely died hard. I set down my hairbrush and turned towards the sound of the door opening. "How did your mission debriefing with Harrison go?" I didn't have to force the bright, intrigued tone to my voice. It was genuine and not a product of the 'always ask about your man's day' teachings my mother raised me on.

"Funny you should mention debriefing," Darren teased, as he stripped down to just his boxer shorts in record time. The rest of his clothes ended up in a pile on the floor. I resisted the urge to remind him to use the clothes basket. As much as I stayed here, which was nearly every night, it was still his room, so his rules. He did not need me to turn into a naggy girlfriend. The mere fact we had reached the point of calling this strange, new, and wonderful gift between us a relationship still made me smile. I had my first boyfriend in one hundred years … and he was a descendant of my last boyfriend. The less I thought of that, the better. Daniel's death was still an ache that no amount of time could completely heal.

"I'm being serious." I covered my mouth to hide my amused smile at his antics. "Was Harrison pleased with the results of the mission?"

Darren shrugged. "The more supplies we have, mean the less Heartsong and his cronies have, so it's a win-win for our side." He sat on the edge of the bed and held out a hand towards me in a silent supplication to join him. I crossed the room and sat sideways across his lap. I wrapped my arms around his neck to steady myself as his hands rested low on my hips. "You were incredible out there tonight. I'm sorry you have to face off against your friends and former clan members, but—for the record—I'm glad we have you on our side. The girls and Parker are proving to be a little more useful than I first thought too."

"There's nowhere else I'd rather be." I rested my head on his shoulder and slid one hand down his chest to his heart. His pulse beat strong and hearty against my fingers. It was the quiet moments such as these that made me miss being alive. I would not trade my afterlife for the death I had planned, and nearly succeeded at, all those years ago, but I missed the thought of growing old and dying a natural death.

Most people wished to turn back the hands of time. I wished the opposite. I was eternally young, but at what price? Living on, while those you love die around you is not an easy task.

"Do you miss him?" Darren had figured out, rather quickly, that when I was at my quietest, it was often because I was thinking of Daniel.

"Miss who?" I attempted to avoid the question.

"You know who," he said, not letting the subject drop. "Great-uncle Daniel."

I sighed. "What gave it away?"

"You're quiet, but it's more than that," he showed off his perceptiveness. "There's a sadness sometimes that nothing can touch. Let me in. I can take it."

"You are one of the strongest people I know," I agreed. "But you should not have to shoulder the burden of my past. That is mine alone."

"Would talking about him help?"

"It might."

"Then tell me about him." Darren unconsciously dug his fingers into my hips, making it hard for me to concentrate. "Tell me something no one else knows."

"You should qualify that statement with 'no one else alive knows.'" I shifted until we were facing each other and wrapped my legs around his waist. That *definitely* helped neither of our concentration levels. The need to kiss Darren and forget everything and everyone but him was overwhelming. I barely controlled the need in favor of continuing my trip through my human memories.

"I was your great-great-grandfather's schoolteacher," I admitted. "He was also named Darren and was the worst pupil. Quite the terror."

"Sounds like I inherited that," Darren joked before trying to keep his face serious and hold his 'I'm listening' expression awhile longer.

I kissed the tip of his nose. "I was seventeen and Darren was twelve. It is near impossible to be taken seriously as a teacher when you are only five years older than some of your students."

"He probably thought you were hot," Darren offered.

"Oh, hush." I ducked my head to hide my blush. "After one particularly disastrous day, I kept Darren after school as punishment. Daniel came to collect him that afternoon, and that is how we met."

"So, great-great-grandpa gets detention, and his brother gets the girl? Typical."

"We had five years together until the Great War took him from me." I pushed the worst of the memories as far out of my mind as I could muster. "Does it bother you that I still keep his picture?"

Darren tilted his head to the side, considering his answer. "He was important to you. I keep that picture of my parents around. It's my way of honoring their memories. Kinda like how keeping Great-uncle Daniel's picture is your way of honoring his memory."

I nodded, near tears. "Thank you for understanding."

Darren's hands curved around my hips to cup my bottom. "So, uh, to sleep or not to sleep?"

"Not to sleep," I decided before leaning in for a kiss.

CHAPTER FOUR

DARREN

EDITH CURLED INTO MY SHOULDER, RESTING HER head against me as she trailed her fingers down my bare chest. I wanted to focus on her, on the feel of her body against mine and the way she let out little growls of pleasure when I squeezed her ass, but all this talk about dead relatives and holding onto memories was proving to be a mood killer. Not that I didn't want her to feel comfortable admitting this stuff to me. Whatever this relationship was going to be, for however long it lasted, I wanted to be the man she needed. But I hadn't thought about my parents in a long time. As we lay there in the stillness, my mind replayed the terror of that night so many years ago.

Smoke clogged my lungs, rousing me from sleep. I could hear something snap above me and I opened my eyes just in time to see the beam over my bed break away from the rest of the ceiling. I scrambled out of bed, hitting the floor with a hard thump as the beam landed where I'd lain seconds ago.

"Danny? Mom? Dad!" I coughed out.

No response.

I raced to the door, forgetting everything I'd ever learned in school about fire safety. Panic was taking over, filling my veins with adrenaline and the overwhelming need to get out. I clawed at the bedroom door, and, when I finally wrenched it open, the hallway was in flames.

"Darren!" Danny's voice was a whisper beneath the flames, and I threw myself towards his bedroom.

I had to believe mom and dad would get out fine. They were adults. They knew what to do in situations like this. I staggered blindly through the heat, my t-shirt and boxers growing slick with grimy sweat. I finally reached the door to his room, but the handle was too hot to touch.

"I'm coming," I tried to yell out to him, but the smoke swallowed my voice.

"Darren, are you all right?" Edith's soft tone brought me back to the present.

I blinked, the room coming back into focus. I could feel the sweat slicking my bare skin. "Sorry, just, uh, kind of got lost for a second," I mumbled.

"Where did you go?"

I could lie to her, but there was no reason to do that. After what we'd been through, we had to be honest with each other. Secrets get people hurt or killed. "My parents, the night they died. I guess talking about Daniel brought things back."

She propped herself up on one elbow, gripped my chin in her hand and turned my face to look at her. "Forgive me for making you relive such painful memories. I did not mean to do so."

I shook my head, trying to ward off her concern. "It's not your fault. It's not like you set the fire."

"Do you know what happened; how it started?"

So much for the promise of a good time as the sun came up. I studied the tiny webs of scars on my knuckles. They were barely visible most of the time. But now they looked fresh and pale against the rest of my skin. "The Hunters that found us said they'd been tracking vampires, and one of them spotted a vamp near our house right before it happened. I never knew which specific vampire did the deed."

She opened her mouth to speak but stopped before any words came out. Her brow knit together, and she wouldn't meet my gaze. "What is it? What do you know?" I couldn't keep the demanding tone in check. She flinched at my words, like I'd slapped her.

"I suspected, but I have no hard proof …" she trailed off.

"What? Edith, just tell me."

"Before we ever met, I went to your home. Crossed paths with Dan when he was a little boy. I went there again the night your parents died. I'd heard there'd been a fire. I was told there were no survivors. It's why I was so surprised when we met months ago at the recruitment weekend."

"Who told you?" My voice had turned icy. I had my suspicions, but I needed her to say the words.

"Mr. Heartsong. He told me you all died."

My knuckles cracked as my fingers contorted into fists. "I'm going to end that murderous piece of shit."

"I'm sorry, Darren. I feel like it is partly my fault." She pushed herself away from me, like she couldn't stand to be near me.

"You didn't tell him to murder innocent people," I answered.

"No, but you were … an impediment to his aims."

Her words took too long to compute in my brain. I knew Heartsong had messed with her memory to make her think I was the enemy. Fuck if I knew what else he'd done to her. But he had been very fixated on her, specifically. Even during the recruitment weekend, he'd been focused on cutting all of her ties to our family.

"He's been trying to fuck you since he turned you, hasn't he?" I spat.

Something in her expression changed. Her eyes went glossy and for a good minute she was somewhere else. She blinked, her gaze still unfocused as she scrambled away from me, trying to cover herself with anything she could find.

"Don't touch me. Please, don't," she whimpered. She wasn't looking at me. Whatever, or whoever, she saw, was the only thing in her mind.

Chapter Five

EDITH

"Don't touch me," My voice was more forceful as my mind hurled me into the past.

"Have you forgotten, my dear, that my touch saved your life? Without me, you would be a corpse in a river. Just a name in the obituary page, waiting for time and memory to forget your very existence. I gave you life, Edith. You should thank me, not—"

"No." I backed against the wall as Mr. Heartsong advanced. "My life had a purpose before you turned me. My afterlife has purpose as well, with or without you."

Mr. Heartsong placed his hands on either side of my head, trapping me in a prison of his arms. I wanted to scream, but the sound would not rise from my throat. Would anyone come if I screamed? Or would his power over the clan hold their sense of duty hostage as surely as his arms held me hostage against the wall?

"Do you remember that day, Edith, my dear?" he whispered, breath hot on my face. "The day I became a part of you forever?" He flicked my hair away from my neck, examining the faded bite mark that would never disappear, not even one hundred years into my afterlife. "You tasted so good. The sweetest blood I've ever had. Do you remember?"

"Y-You asked if I wished to live t-to do good, and I said yes." I flinched when he placed his mouth against my neck, his fangs scraping against the long-ago pierced skin. "Please don't."

"Are you afraid you may want me as much as I want you?" he asked, his hypnotic voice muddying my senses and dampen-ing my will to fight. My knees sagged a little, but I did not fall.

"I want to go home."

"You are home," he insisted. "I am your home."

"No." I shook my head. "No, there is another."

"There is no one but me."

"Edith?"

I blinked, tumbling back into the present as quickly as I had fallen into the past. "I … I'm sorry, Darren. Please, forgive me."

I grabbed my gauzy robe and pulled it on before fleeing his room into the darkened hall. I did not know where I intended to go. Darren's room was just as much my room now as his. We had given up the pretense of separate quarters months ago.

"Mama E?"

I turned at the sound of Hope's voice. "You should sleep, *Bopha.* We have precious few hours to renew our strength."

She chewed on her bottom lip, refusing to turn around and return to her room. "I know, but I can't."

"What's wrong?" I asked. "Did you have one of your nightmares?"

Hope shook her head. "No. Angel snuck out to see Caden. I know his trigger stuff is supposed to be healed or whatever, but what if it's not? I tried to sleep but all I could think about was what if she's in danger and doesn't even know it? He could stake her, Mama E, and make it look like the clan did it."

I wrapped an arm around her thin shoulders, hoping the gesture offered her a modicum of comfort. "Which way did she go, *Bopha*? We can look for her together."

Hope gestured vaguely down a dark hall leading to an exit. "Outside." She glanced between me and Darren's closed door, her expression turning anxious. "But if you come with … aren't you … um … missing out on … time with Darren?"

"My priority will always be you and your sister," I reassured her. "That doesn't change with an update to my relationship status. Come on. Let's find Angel."

Hope led the way to the heavy exit door. It was propped open slightly to stop it from closing and locking Angel and Caden outside. Could it also be propped open to let someone in? Such as clan members waiting to ambush us in our home base? I shook the thought from my mind and followed Hope outdoors. The moon was incredibly bright, illuminating the shadowy figures of Angel and Caden standing under a nearby tree. I put a hand on Hope's arm to signal her to wait. The teen couple's raised voices floated to us on the cool breeze.

"Why won't you tell me what's really going on, Caden?" Angel accused. "I'm not stupid. You're not 'cured.' If anything, you're worse than before."

"No, I'm not," he insisted. "That's just what the Hunters want you to believe." He reached out to grab her upper arms when she turned to leave. "Keep your friends close and your enemies closer, right? They still think I'm a threat."

"Well, aren't you?"

"No. Not even close. You've got to believe me, Ange—"

"Release her now, Caden," I ordered before stepping into the light with Hope close behind me. The second he grabbed Angel's arm was the second I put a stop to whatever this meeting was. "Go inside, go to bed, and pray I don't tell Darren or his superiors about this."

"Tell them about what?" Caden's hand dropped from Angel's arms all the same. "We were only talking. Tell them, Angel."

"I think you should go inside like Mama E said." Angel turned her face from him. I suspected it was to hide her tears more than showing displeasure at his actions, unfortunately. The girls—especially Angel—only saw what they wanted to see. If she didn't want to believe her boyfriend may very well still be compromised, she wouldn't.

"This is bullshit," Caden muttered, yet stalked past us into the base none-the-less.

Angel ran to me and flung herself into my waiting arms. "I'm sorry, Mama E. I should have told someone where I was going. I just … I thought Caden would talk to me—really talk to me—like he doesn't talk to the doctors or Dan or anyone else who asks him how he is, but he … but he …" She shook her head, her tears wetting my robe and nightgown.

"It's okay, *Bopha*," I soothed. "You care about him. Our hearts make us do reckless things. That's what still makes us human, underneath the vampire."

"Are you mad at me?" She sniffled and took a step back, doing a better job at composing herself than I thought possible after such a charged encounter with Caden.

"No." I smoothed her dark hair back from her face and brow. "But I would like you to promise to not be alone with Caden until the doctors give him a clean bill of health. Can you do that? Just because we've discovered one trigger word, doesn't mean more aren't hiding somewhere in his mind. Your grandsire is a very crafty man. We can't trust him, and, unfortunately, that means we can't fully trust Caden just yet either."

"Can we go inside now?" Angel asked. It was not lost on me she side-stepped the promise not to be alone with Caden.

I walked the girls back to their bedroom, tucked them in as if they were little children, before wandering back towards Darren's room. I paused near his door, unwilling to wake him if he had fallen asleep. He needed rest more than I. Instead of disturbing him, I found my way to the rec room and curled up on one of the couches. It proved a chilly night when I was used to the warmth of Darren's arms, but I could not go back now. Not when the troubling memories of my glamoured two-day return to the clan made me doubt what I once thought was true.

CHAPTER SIX

DARREN

I THOUGHT I HEARD FOOTSTEPS IN THE HALLWAY sometime after Edith ran out, but they retreated before I could investigate. I knew the good boyfriend thing to do was to make sure she was all right, but I'd never been the type to go and comfort anyone. Especially when I didn't know what was going on in her head.

The morning light filtered through the very bottoms of the blackout curtains. Transitioning to sleeping during the day had taken some getting used to, but we were all managing it. With Heartsong and his cronies bringing the war to us, we had to find whatever advantage we could. Edith insisted it was because humans had waged war in the light of day, during the last war, that caused the vampires' downfall. And this was at the forefront of Heartsong's current strategy.

Despite knowing my body needed sleep, I couldn't make my mind slow down and shut off. My worry over Danny pushing himself too far, and too fast, coupled with whatever memory was consuming Edith, made it clear that sleep wasn't coming soon. So, I did what any good Hunter would do. I got off my ass, pulled on pants and a shirt, and crept into the hallway. I padded down the hall towards the stairs to the first floor. The sound of someone else moving around drew my attention.

Everyone should be sleeping now, not roaming the halls. Given how much we'd decimated Heartsong's cronies last night, I doubted we had unwanted company, but years of training took over and I pressed myself to the wall, inching closer to the sound. I reached the corner and peered around it to catch the back of a distinctly male head retreating towards the other end of the hall.

"What are you doing out of your room?" I called to the figure.

He turned. It was Caden sneaking off. If he wanted us to believe he was de-triggered, slinking around when everyone was asleep wasn't the best way to show it. His cheeks fLushed, and he shoved his hands into his pockets.

"I'm not a prisoner," he said as I approached, my hands held at my sides. I had to be ready in case he decided he wasn't totally deprogrammed.

"But you aren't safe, either," I reminded him.

He glared at me. “I don’t know what I have to do to make you all believe me. He’s not controlling me anymore. I tried to get Angel to believe me, but she’s just scared of me. I hate that my girlfriend is scared of me.”

Any retort died on my lips as I looked at him and saw not a danger to my safety, but a scared kid who hadn’t seen his family in months. Did they even know he was still alive? He’d come back to base with us after the recruitment weekend and hadn’t gone home in between, and then he’d gone sleeper agent on us.

“Look, we all know it’s not your fault,” I said. “Heartsong is a manipulative piece of shit and he used you because he knew it would hurt Edith and her girls. You had the misfortune of being involved with the wrong girl at the wrong time.”

He looked up at me, and I caught the glisten of unshed tears. I wouldn’t admit it, but a part of me wanted to hug him and promise it would all be okay. But I wasn’t his family, and I needed people to continue to see me as a leader. Getting mushy in times of war would not ensure people would follow my directives in the field.

“Come with me,” I whispered and started down the stairs. His footfalls trailed mine until we ended up in the train-ing room. He stopped at the bottom of the stairs. “What are we doing down here?”

“Look, I get you’re scared and pissed off. We can’t afford to let you off base, but that doesn’t mean we can’t make sure you’re able to defend yourself without his mind-fuck mojo.”

“Look, Darren, if this is some brotherly pep talk or what-ever, I’m not interested. I don’t fight. It kills me I hurt one of my best friends. I barely remember any of it.”

"Even pacifists need to throw a punch in a pinch. Now, get your ass over here." When he didn't move, I added, "I'm not asking."

He heaved an exaggerated sigh but stalked into the room, holding his hands up in a boxer's stance. "Tell me what you remember about the recruitment weekend," I said and moved around him, my own fists raised.

"I remember them trying to pin a bunch of murders on Dan. They convicted him and you busted him out before they could kill him," Caden responded, shuffling backwards as I took a swing.

"Were you ever alone with Heartsong?" I sent another punch towards his head and he failed to block me completely.

Staggering off balance, he answered, "I don't remember."

"Think harder."

"Why does it matter? We know he messed with my head."

"Because I asked and whether you like it or not, you're under my command. When your superior asks you a question, you answer."

"We aren't military," he grumbled.

"Wrong," I retorted, and landed a kick to his solar plexus.

He crumbled under the weight of the blow, dropping his hands and pressing them to his stomach. "Now, tell me if you were ever alone with him."

"I … only when I first got there," Caden gasped. "He saw me with Hope and Angel. He introduced himself and told me he was excited to have such open-minded people attending." His face screwed up in concentration. "Then, I was back with everyone and you showed up. But, after dinner, the girls told me I'd been off with him for like twenty minutes."

Less than half an hour seemed too short a time to implant such specific skills and instructions in his head, and yet Heartsong had convinced Edith that I was the enemy and nearly erased me from her memory. But that took two days. He was fucking ancient and far more powerful than I'd given him credit for. And if my suspicions were right, he'd at least ordered the hit on my family.

Caden continued to gasp, but I kept my distance. He shot me an annoyed look as he tried to straighten, wincing as he did so. "I'm not going to be triggered."

A short amount of testing wasn't conclusive or definitive proof he was safe to be out in the field again, but it was better than nothing. "I had to be sure. Why don't you get some sleep," I replied and clapped him on the shoulder before using my own momentum to push him towards the stairs ahead of me.

He might not think he's a threat anymore, but that didn't mean I wanted to turn my back on him just yet.

With any luck, we'd both be headed for unconsciousness soon with nothing but empty blackness in our dreams. But who was I kidding, I'm not that fucking lucky.

CHAPTER SEVEN

EDITH

SLEEP ELUDED ME. THE COUCH WAS TOO HARD, and my mind was too full. I lay awake and watched the sun rise through the skylight in the rec room. Were the memories that surfaced from my recent glamoured return to the clan real? Or just another trick played by Mr. Heartsong, to wreak havoc on all who defied him? Tricks, games, and pettiness were his lifeblood. That wasn't news or a secret to anyone in the clan. He tempered those reprehensible qualities with charisma and rhetoric that always put doubts to rest … if only for a little while.

Once I was out of that orbit—frankly, that cult—I could see him clearly for what he was, more monster than man. The question that still lingered was *why?* Why would my sire focus so much of his energy on the Paxton family? The only answer that made sense, was *me.* He hated them because they stood in the way of my full commitment to the clan. All the Paxtons from Daniel straight on down to Darren and Dan stood in the way of my full commitment to *him.*

"Why didn't I see it sooner?"

I stood up. The morning sun lit the way, as I crept back to the bedroom where I still kept a small portion of my belongings. I dressed in a knee-length, red cotton dress, and pulled a light jacket over the top, so to hide my fountain pen up my sleeve. I grew up in an era where ladies wore skirts or dresses, and no amount of modern living could break me from that habit. I at least adjusted from ankle and calf length to knee-length. Knee-length dresses and skirts did not impede movement as much in a fight. For a second, I thought of waking Darren, but he would not want to come where I was going. I barely wanted to go myself.

I slipped out of the Hunter base undetected and turned east into the rising sun. I knew the way to where I intended to go well, even though it had been years since I last visited the site of the Paxton family fire. The city had razed what was left of the house soon after the fire, but no one had ever built anything in its place. It remained an empty lot. Perhaps Darren and Dan still owned the land and did not want to see a new house in its place. I never thought to ask, since, until recently, I believed the boys deceased as well.

The lot was deserted when I reached my destination. The grass was neatly mowed, not overgrown or abandoned at all. A small wooden cross memorial stood in the middle of what was once the location of the kitchen. I inched closer, memories of a time when this spot was filled with laughter and love overwhelming me. PAXTON was written on the horizontal portion of the cross in Darren's handwriting. I sunk to my knees, touching each letter as if it would somehow bring the brothers' parents back. As if my will alone could turn back time and erase what was already done.

"Of course, I knew I would find you here. You are so predictable, Edith my dear." I turned at the sound of Mr. Heartsong's voice, ratcheting to my feet and sliding my weapon into my hand in one fluid motion. "Murderer."

Mr. Heartsong shrugged. "Come now, Edith, you know I don't like to muddy my hands with such trivial matters, when I have lackeys to do that for me. You should have known I'd never let them live."

"Trivial matters?" I spat. "Good people died."

"Good people die all the time," he pointed out. "What makes this family any different?"

"They were *my* family." I clutched my deadly fountain pen tighter in my fist. "They were all I ever wanted in this entire world."

"And that, my dear, was the problem." Mr. Heartsong stuck his hands in his pockets and slowly circled me like a beast contemplating its prey. "Have you not figured it out in all this time? Your attachment was their downfall. The one thing I ask of clan members is to renounce all ties to their human existence."

"Only to control us better," I accused. "What's a cult without loyal followers?"

He tilted his head to the side as he contemplated my words. "A cult? Is that how you see us now? We're family, Edith. We could be more than that, if you'd only give in to the inevitable."

"Never." I spun towards him, hoping to gain the element of surprise as I raised my weapon. Mr. Heartsong stepped aside as if I was moving in slow motion. I stumbled but did not fall, barely keeping hold of my pen, and not staking myself at the same time.

"Pity," he clucked. "We are a pair, Edith. You just need more time to come to that realization. I am patient, my dear, but even my patience wears thin."

"I am nothing like you, and I will never 'pair' with you," I vowed.

"Oh, my dear, don't you remember?" His smile grew sinister. "You already have."

My weapon clattered from my hand at his words. "Wh-what do you mean?"

"Search your memories—the hazy ones, from when you returned to us," he said. "The truth is waiting there. I'd made it hard for them to surface for you until now. It is ever so much more fun to watch the destruction of your ties to the Paxtons over a long period, versus all at once. Wouldn't you agree?"

My knees trembled, and I tumbled to the ground. Mr. Heartsong leaned over me, that same sinister grin that I knew could mean anything, spread across his features. I stared into his gaunt face, unsure what he planned to do. Kill me? Kiss me? Something else entirely?

"You're mine, Edith my dear," he said. "I will not let that foolish human with an overdeveloped sense of vengeance take you from me."

I opened my mouth to respond, but he was gone before any words came out, leaving as suddenly as he appeared. What secrets did my repressed memories hold? Was Mr. Heartsong toying with me, or was there truth mixed in with his lies?

CHAPTER EIGHT

DARREN

WORRIES OVER EDITH CONSUMED MY thoughts, keeping sleep at bay. After lying in bed without luck for nearly an hour, I grunted, got dressed and traipsed into the hall. I could compensate for the lack of sleep with coffee and a protein bowl. But I needed to make sure Edith was okay. I crept down the hall, like I had only a short time ago, stopping at the room Hope and Angel shared. I nudged the door open with my toe, just enough to catch sight of them both snoring in their beds.

Retreating, I made quick work of checking on Caden. He was sprawled across the bed, face down on the pillow. At least he got some sleep. He hadn't asked for any of this and yet, here he was, stuck in the middle of a maniacal vampire's war. I was about to head downstairs when I heard sounds coming from Danny's room. My brother was a heavy sleeper, and it would take a bomb going off to rouse him these days. *So why was he up?*

I paused outside the door, trying to pick apart the sounds coming through, but my brain was too tired. I didn't believe he was in any danger, but he'd pushed himself yesterday, more than he should have, and he could have re-injured himself. I grabbed the doorknob and twisted, shoving the door inward with more force than necessary.

I immediately regretted the decision. Danny lay in bed in just his boxers, Parker beside him in a similar state of undress, his hand dangerously close to the hem of my brother's underwear.

"What the hell, Darren?" Danny snapped, reaching for the first thing he could throw at me.

I dodged the knee brace with ease.

"I heard noises, I got worried," I replied, already backing out of the room.

"Get out, douchebag!" he growled.

I wasted no more time leaving. Theoretically, I understood Danny's relationship with Parker. Or at least what he wanted it to be. Until recently, Parker had been too uptight to even hold Danny's hand. And now they were about to …

"Use protection!" I shouted through the door. Another thump resounded as he threw something else.

Trying to scrub the mental image from my mind, I raced down to the kitchen, hoping I'd find Edith there pouring blood into her coffee. It was empty. I set the pot to brew and checked the rec room. The fabric on the couch cushions were rumpled. Someone had definitely been here, and not that long ago.

My gut told me Edith wasn't on the base, and that was problematic. Whatever had set her off, I knew it was because of Heartsong. Whenever shit got complicated with us, it was his fault. I was not deflecting blame. It was just a fact. But, if she'd gone off chasing memories, that left a lot of places to check. And far too many openings for her to get caught by the enemy.

Throwing together what I called a protein bowl—deli ham, eggs, cheese, and some protein powder—I ate it in under five minutes. I downed the coffee in just as quick a time before grabbing the keys to the van and heading out. I could have told someone I was leaving, but this felt less like a mission and more like protecting my family. Sometimes, it still amazed me that Edith fell into that category, after such a short time in each other's lives.

But then, I've been in her life a lot longer than a few months. She admitted as much when we first met. She'd kept tabs on the family that was almost hers before Daniel's death during the war. All she'd ever wanted was to be part of the Paxton line. No matter what bullshit Heartsong had put in her head when he'd lured her back to the clan, she'd never forgotten that desire.

I climbed behind the wheel of the van, gunned the engine, and pressed the gas pedal to the floor. I shot out of the lot behind base, and onto the busy city streets. We may be at war, but the rest of the world was blissfully unaware. Or they thought it was all a big joke. The government hadn't even bothered to call in the National Guard or anything. We'd been waging a war under everyone's noses and it made me wonder if that was how vampires had to live their afterlives, so under the radar that Hunters wouldn't spot them.

I'd never love all vampires, but I'd realized they were people, and, like people, there were some out there, who didn't want to tear apart humanity. I focused on that as I drove a route I hadn't done in months. Not since before Edith and I met. It didn't take long to find the plot of land that used to be our house. Danny didn't know I paid someone to keep it looking decent and the grass cut. We'd lost so much in this place, it didn't need to look the part of the ugly reminder of death and destruction.

I rolled to a stop across the street to find Edith sitting in the grass, head in her hands. I left the engine running as I climbed out and crossed the empty street. I stopped before I got too close to her, not wanting to freak her out if she was lost in a memory.

"Edith," I called.

Her head whipped around at the sound of my voice, and she wiped bluish tears from her cheeks. "How did you find me?"

"I tracked your phone," I said with a smirk. Her face transformed with confusion. I added, "I figured if you were going down memory lane, you might come here."

She stood and brushed stray bits of grass and dirt from her dress. “He was here. He said things … Darren, I am so sorry about earlier, but I think there may be some things I have not yet dealt with from my return to the clan.” She stepped up to me and placed shaking hands on my chest. “I beg you to be patient with me.”

“I’m here. I don’t run from a fight. Not when the bastard on the other end is going after my family.”

She gave me a sad smile. “I think perhaps that desire for family has led us all here to the brink of disaster.”

“I won’t let him hurt you again.” I guided her to the waiting van.

She climbed into the passenger seat and I rounded the hood, casting a glance around the neighborhood, but I didn’t sense anyone watching us. That didn’t mean Heartsong wasn’t somewhere nearby. I’d better take the scenic route back.

“How do you feel about making a quick detour before we go home?” I said and buckled the belt across my lap.

“Where?”

“The place we should have had our first date.”

CHAPTER NINE

EDITH

DARREN PARKED IN FRONT OF A SMALL, RETRO diner tucked away in midtown between soaring modern buildings. From the outside, it gave off a quaint, come-in-to-forget-your-troubles vibe, that so many diners and soda shops did in the 1950s. Today, that would just be considered nostalgia, but I remembered living through that decade.

Darren shut off the van, pocketed the keys, and hopped down with a litheness that still made my body ache in anticipation, no matter how mundane the task at hand. Walking around the van to open my door, and offering me a hand should not be sexy, yet his ease of movement made it so … at least to me.

"Thank you." I remembered my manners as I took his hand and climbed down. Darren shifted his hand to the small of my back, once my feet were firmly on the ground, and propelled us into the diner. Inside was just as cheery as I'd hoped, with bright chrome counters and tabletops, and neon lights. Music filled the small space. I smiled. It felt so good to smile after being on edge for so long.

"What can I get you, honey?" A waitress approached us, her hair tied in an impossibly high ponytail and her uniform not as modest as it should be if she was trying to emulate the 1950s. Perhaps she was hoping for more Bettie Page and less Doris Day. The way her gaze rested on Darren was as if I did not exist. It instantly told me he had caught her eye before. I clamped down on the thin spiral of jealousy before it threatened to ruin our quiet afternoon. I needed quiet. I needed a normal date.

"Hey … Lorraine." Darren's eyes flicked to her name tag. He was rather terrible with names, but the gesture came off as looking at her overstuffed push-up bra, versus needing a reminder on what to call her. "I promised my girl here Pop's famous chicken and waffles. Can you help us out on that front?"

"Sure, honey." Lorraine led the way to an empty booth. She leaned over more than was necessary to set the menus down before *accidentally* backing into Darren. I don't think I imagined the extra little hip grind she did before stepping away. "Oops, sorry honey. I didn't see you there."

"We don't need menus." Darren ignored her blatant come on. "Chicken and waffles, and coffee for both of us."

Lorraine nodded, not bothering to write down the order. It wouldn't surprise me if my half never appeared, or, if it did, was mysteriously burned. Not that Lorraine was waitressing and cooking, but she could have a word with the cook.

"I don't trust her," I announced as we sat down across from each other. "She doesn't like me."

"She didn't say a single word to you." Darren made a tower out of the sugar packets instead of looking at me. He seemed nervous. I tilted my head to the side, watching him.

"When was the last time you were on a proper date?"

The jelly packets joined the sugars in Darren's condiment construction. "Uh, where I had to talk to someone instead of going straight to the good part? Maybe high school?"

"Which was how many years ago?" My eyes widened when I realized something I failed to ask him until now. "I have no idea how old you are."

Darren grinned. That charming, disarming grin could make me follow him anywhere and forgive nearly anything. "I'm twenty-four. How old were you before …?"

"Was turned?" I finished the sentence for him. "Twenty-two. Though, if we were going strictly by birth year, I would be one-hundred and twenty-two."

"Let's not." Darren made a face when he took a swig of the black coffee that had made it to our table in a timely fashion. He poured some of his sugar packets into it before drinking more. "Go by birth year, I mean. You're twenty-two. That's good enough for me."

"But you won't always be twenty-four."

"Not unless some vamp bites me and then I'd sta—" Darren stopped short when he realized what he was about to say. "Then I'd say, 'no thank you' and keep having birthdays. Why don't we celebrate yours?"

"I don't enjoy reminders of time passing." The coffee tasted bitter without a touch of blood in it, but I drank it anyway.

"No one likes getting older, but it's part of life." Darren reached across the table and grabbed my hand. "Next year, you're turning twenty-three. Promise."

"If there is a next year."

"Heartsong won't win." Darren knew where my thoughts wandered without me having to tell him. "We won't let him."

"I appreciate your optimism."

Lorraine returned with the food, setting Darren's down in front of him first. She leaned over too far again, until I was quite positive her breasts were going to fall out of her push-up bra. They stayed put by some miracle of gravity. She slid my plate across the table to me. The chicken and waffles looked surprisingly edible.

"Let me know if you need anything," she said to Darren. "And I mean anything."

"Thanks, Lorraine, we're good." Darren loaded up a forkful of chicken and waffles together after Lorraine skulked away. He held it out to me, not in a couple's 'feed each other' way but as a demonstration on the proper way to eat Pop's specialty. "See, the magic to chicken and waffles, is to load them up together. Not waffle or chicken first. Both at the same time." He motioned at me. "Go on. You try."

I followed his example. "Like this?"

Darren nodded. "Now all in at once. No lady like nibble or whatever shit your mom raised you on. I bring you to a diner, I expect you to eat."

I stuffed the whole forkful of food into my mouth and chewed. It was, like he said, heavenly. How had I lived so long without discovering this taste combination?

"Good, right?" Darren asked, watching my food ecstasy from across the table.

"Divine," I agreed. "I think it's the best thing I've ever had in my mouth … well, food at least."

Darren choked on his coffee before spitting it back into his cup. "Warn a guy the next time you tell a dirty joke. On the plus side, I think I finally corrupted the ladylike Edith Dorset." He saluted me with his cup. "And it only took a little over three months. Am I good or what?"

"The best," I played along. "Though, I don't know if you want to claim corrupting women as your superpower."

He shrugged. "I can't help what I'm good at."

We smiled at each other, neither of us keeping a straight face for long, before dissolving into laughter. For the first time, in a long time, I felt young and carefree. At this moment, I was just a girl on a date with her boyfriend, and not a vampire on the human side of a civil war.

"What's your middle name?" I asked, wanting to hold on to this sense of normalcy for as long as possible.

"Don't have one," Darren replied. "What's yours?"

"Elenor," I said. "Edith Elenor Dorset. How's that for ladylike?"

"I like it. It suits you," Darren said, around a mouthful of food.

I felt heat rise in my cheeks. I couldn't remember the last time I blushed over a silly compliment. I opened my mouth to respond when the sounds of breaking glass shattered our sense of peace. The sound of screaming diner patrons, mixed with the unmistakable hiss of vampires baring their fangs followed as more and more vampires climbed through the jagged plate-glass window, ready for a fight.

Acting on instinct, Darren dived under the table and pulled me with him. "Don't move." He flicked his wrist to engage the constant stake hidden inside his arm strap. "There's too many of them. If we surprise 'em, we might get ourselves and the others out alive. I'm going in."

I grabbed his arm before he could leave me behind. "Not without me."

He sighed, looking like he wanted to argue before saying, "On three, then?"

I nodded. "On three."

"One. Two. Three."

CHAPTER TEN

DARREN

THE STAKE IN MY HAND FELT LIKE A NATURAL extension of my body as I rushed out from under the table. People screamed, and I blocked out the sound. My gaze focused on the ringleader of these bloodsucking assholes. He wore a tight leather jacket with a mohawk that wasn't cool even in the 80s. The bright green tips were like a neon sign, begging me to "Look Here."

Maybe that was his plan and my mistake. Because, as I charged him, he whipped out something small from his jacket pocket and a bolt of electricity danced along every nerve ending in my body. The stake dropped from my hand as my fingers seized. I tipped against a nearby chair and sent it skidding across the room as my body slumped.

I gritted my teeth hard, trying to avoid biting my tongue as I got my body under control. Green Mohawk advanced on me, fangs bared as he grinned wickedly.

"Not so tough now, are you, Hunter?" he snarled, his fetid breath wafting over my face.

"Fuck you," I growled.

"Now, now, there are ladies here," he chided and moved to backhand me.

Every muscle in my body ached in protest as I brought up a hand to block him. As he leaned closer, I could see the fresh blood on his tongue and lips. He'd fed recently, and he wanted me to know it. I connected with his hand and used his momentum against him, sending him flying back into the booth behind me. I struggled to my feet, reclaimed my stake, and lobbed it at his back. It penetrated the leather of his jacket and sunk into flesh, but he moved and my body was sore. It cost me my usual precision.

"My jacket!" Mohawk howled and clawed at his back, trying to dislodge the stake.

Edith remained under the table until that moment. She snaked her arm up and seized it, slamming it home through the front of his body.

He gave a garbled cry and fell flat on the floor. Everyone in the room seemed to wait with bated breath. He stopped moving but didn't turn to ash. He was too young for that.

I ripped the stake from his chest and spun to face his buddies.

"You sure you want to come at me, boys?" I called.

I heard Edith move to stand beside me and, given the slight hiss, I suspected she was reminding them she was just as strong, if not stronger. I watched as a couple of the vampires hesitated before rushing, not at us, but at the remaining patrons and staff. One of them looped an arm around Lorraine's throat, holding her close. She screamed. That seemed to spurn his buddies on, and the others fanned out, tackling people. Another shout came from the kitchen as a vampire dragged the cook out of the kitchen by the scruff of his neck.

"You're outnumbered, Hunter. You can't take us all on," the vampire holding Lorraine taunted, pressing his mouth to her throat.

She squirmed, her breasts bouncing provocatively in her uniform top. *Why was I staring at her breasts?* I hated to admit he was right. Edith and I made a good team, but these bastards had the element of surprise and we weren't nearly armed well enough. And I doubted they would chill and let Edith and I come up with a plan of attack.

"Who sent you?" Edith's voice was calm, lilting.

"Why should we answer you, traitor?" a vampire in the back shouted.

Whether he realized it or not, he gave away the identity of their true ringleader. Had Heartsong been lingering around the site of the fire? Had he followed us here? I didn't have time to worry about it now. We had to get these people out of here safely. I bent down and kicked at a nearby chair leg until it broke off, tossing it to Edith, who caught it one-handed without taking her eyes off the cluster of vampires.

"Help me," Lorraine moaned.

I glanced sideways to see a thick trail of blood leaking down her chest. A nasty gash marred her throat. The vampire had taken a bite and probably ripped her jugular vein. If we didn't get pressure on it, she was going to bleed out and fast.

Edith's nose twitched, and in the time it took me to breathe, she had taken out the vampire holding Lorraine, and laid her on the ground, one hand pressed to her throat.

With the vampires momentarily distracted by yet more of their numbers being taken off the board, I took my chance. I got a running start, flinging knives at as many as I could. All landed with a meet thump into hearts that barely beat. The sudden decrease in threat seemed to spur the rest of the customers on. Those who could, grabbed chairs and dull butter knives, taking up arms against these intruders of their nice, quiet breakfasts.

Not expecting to fight a diner full of pissed off people, the vampires scattered, darting out of the broken front window. I slumped to the floor at Edith's side.

"She'll need a hospital. There is only so much I can do here," Edith whispered softly.

I glanced over my shoulder, trying to find anyone who might reach for a cell phone. I saw an older woman pulling one out of an oversized purse. I pointed at her. "You. Call 911. This woman needs an ambulance. Now!"

Maybe it was Lorraine's blood covering my hands, but she dialed the phone and I listened long enough to hear her give the address to the dispatcher. Lorraine's gaze was already unfocused.

"Stay with us," I said, gripping her hand. She squeezed back weakly.

"They knew we were here," hissed Edith.

"Your stalker," I muttered.

We were going to have to come up with alternative routes to and from the base. If he'd been able to follow us here, he could find us anywhere, and I won't let some madman with a God complex come bursting into my home, and put the people I love at risk.

But sticking around there wasn't safe either. The police hadn't been getting involved in Hunter business so far, but this was a public attack. "We need to go before the police show up," I told Edith.

"But, won't they need to take our statements?"

"We're not exactly a sanctioned government operation. As far as they know, we don't even exist. They don't want to believe this war is going on. And I won't sit around and be questioned about dropping a fuck ton of bodies in front of witnesses."

The cook appeared over my left shoulder, held out a clean cloth and knelt down. "Go. I'll take care of her. You saved our lives."

I didn't know if Lorraine was going to make it, but I didn't have time to argue semantics with the man. He was giving us an out, and I grabbed Edith's hand, pulling her along behind me and out of the diner, just as sirens wailed and lights flashed at the end of the street.

CHAPTER ELEVEN

EDITH

I DUG MY HEELS IN, FORCING DARREN TO JERK TO a halt outside the van. He glared over his shoulder at me, appearing more tired and in pain than I expected, as the adrenaline of the fight wore off.

"You need medical," I said.

"I'm fine," he snapped.

I flinched at his harsh tone. "Do not take your frustrations out on me. In case you failed to remember, this spot was your idea in the—"

Darren forked his free hand through his hair, that was already sticking up slightly, from the electric current the vampire's taser sent through him. "You've got to be fucking kidding me. Are we seriously fighting right now? Just get in the damn van, Edith."

I tilted my chin up in defiance. "No."

He narrowed his eyes. "What do you mean, no?"

"I mean exactly that." I pulled my hand free of his. There was little resistance. "I refuse to get in the van until you agree to get medical attention. The clans are fighting dirty. Based on your symptoms, there was more than just electricity in that taser. It would not surprise me if they'd laced it with something else. Perhaps a nerve agent."

"I'm fine," Darren insisted. He fumbled for the van keys in his pocket, and dropped them three times in the parking lot, before finally getting a firm enough grip, to open the van's back doors. "Now get in."

"Agree to medical first."

He scowled, looking like he wished to argue more before finally saying, "Fine."

"Thank you." I climbed in and crawled through the back of the van to the seats up front. Darren shut the doors. He should have come into view to get into the driver's seat, but he never appeared. "Darren?" My worry made me move at lightning speed. I found him slumped against the front tire of the van. His arms and legs lay at useless odd angles, like a marionette with its strings cut. "Can you move at all?"

He tried to shake his head, but even that ended with his head lolling to the side. "You're going to have to drive." Each word was a struggle. I forced down my fear and panic over Darren's health, balling my hands into fists to hide the shaking.

"I don't know how to drive," I reminded him. "I never learned."

"Now's a good a time as any."

I rested a hand against his chest, trying to make it look as if it were a comforting gesture, when really, I was checking to see if his heart was slowing down, as whatever nerve agent the clan put on that taser worked its way through his body. His heartbeat was slow and steady. The steady was a good sign. I wasn't so sure what the slow meant yet. "Let's get you off the ground first. Then we'll talk about driving lessons."

I plucked the van keys from the floor before wrapping Darren's arm around my shoulders and hauling him to his feet. It would be easier to get him into the back of the van than the passenger front seat. I ignored his protests as I unlocked the back door and pulled us both inside. The police cars, fire truck, and ambulance had descended onto the diner. We were safe for now, hiding in the windowless interior of the van. I hated to think of it as *hiding*, but the last thing we needed was to be interrogated by any law enforcement agencies. With luck, the diner patrons would forget our role in the violence. It was too late and too taxing to attempt a mass glamour.

"You could call Danny," Darren suggested, as I helped him onto the mattress used for overnight reconnaissance missions. "Any vamps still hanging around are looking for us, not him."

"He can't drive due to his knee injury, remember?" I flashed a tight-lipped smile to cover my rising fear. "It has to be me." I scrambled over the console into the driver's seat. It felt foreign and unnatural to me. "Now which side is the brake, and which is the gas?" I asked.

Darren swore under his breath but managed to sound positive when he answered, "Brake is on the left, gas on the right. You know how to turn the van on, right?"

"Sort of," I said, as I stuck the key in the ignition and turned it towards me. Nothing happened. I turned it the other way, and the engine sprung to life. "What next?"

"Put your foot on the brake, then move the gearshift into D for drive. Slowly move your foot off the brake and onto the gas. I pulled through on the parking spot so you can just go forward. No need to back up."

The van lurched and jerked down the street for about a block before I stopped at a stop sign. "What now?"

"Nothing. You're so-called driving is making us look suspicious as hell." His words ended on a hiss of pain.

"I told you I couldn't drive."

"And I told you to call Danny."

I made an awkward turn down the street to the right of the stop sign and shut off the van. "Let's compromise. I'll call Parker. Dan will surely come with him."

Darren thought it over for a moment before snapping, "Fine."

I dug my new cellular phone out of my small purse. I hated technology—especially cellular phones—but Darren and the girls insisted I needed one. They also insisted I always carry it with me in case of emergencies. This definitely constituted an emergency. Darren and the girls had picked out a simple phone where I only had to hit a specific number, to call a specific person. Parker was number five on the list. He picked up on the third ring.

"Edith?"

"Parker, I can't explain everything now, but there was an ambush at Pop's Diner in midtown," I said in a rush. "Darren was injured. I can't drive the van. We need you and Dan."

"We're on our way," Parker said without hesitation, and ended the call.

I climbed into the back of the van and sat next to Darren on the mattress. Under different circumstances, he'd probably tease me about there being a mattress and we shouldn't miss an opportunity when it's handed to us. Instead, I clutched my sharp fountain pen in my hand, ready to defend us if needed, and hoping we made it out of here alive.

"Please hurry," I whispered out loud. "I don't know how much longer he has until the nerve agent completely takes hold."

CHAPTER TWELVE

DARREN

I COULD STILL HEAR EDITH BESIDE ME, SENDING up a prayer that I'd survive. I had been so busy focusing on taking out the vamps in the diner, I hadn't realized that they'd laced the damn taser with anything. I didn't even know you could *do* that.

Somehow, I expected to be in a wild panic, yet as I lay there on the mattress, my body going numb from the top down, I wasn't scared. I was just so damn tired. I'd joined this fight so long ago, dedicated myself to it because I wanted to get back at the monsters who took my family away from me. But buried somewhere deep down, I always assumed I'd go out fighting. Maybe protecting Danny or some other Hunter or some random civilian who couldn't defend themselves. But I'd always assumed there would be an end point.

Since meeting Edith, I'd pushed that fatalistic expectation down deeper still. I had something to live for now. Someone who gave a crap about what happened to me. Because she didn't want to be alone in this world either.

"Darren, can you still hear me?" Edith's face hovered above mine, her hair dripping into her eyes as she pressed a cool palm to my cheek. At least I assumed that's what she'd done. I'd lost sensation in my face.

"Feels … fuzzy," I got out through tingling lips.

"Help is coming," she said, tears in her eyes.

"Always knew …" I tried to get out, but she shook her head. "Save your strength."

I worried if I succumbed to the darkness, I'd never claw my way back out. And I wasn't sure I would want to fight it, either. Heartsong had been playing the long game. So far back, none of us were even a blip on the radar. Someone somewhere had wronged him so deeply he'd held a grudge for centuries against the rest of humanity.

I forced myself to swallow and tried to speak again. "If I don't—," I began, but she was there again, pressing her lips to mine. I couldn't feel the sensation of them, but I knew the memory of them, and it was almost enough to trick my brain into believing I could feel their weight.

"None of that talk now," she chided when she pulled away.

I wanted to shake my head, but that took more muscle control and coordination than I had. "Need to say this," I huffed. "If I don't make it … I need you to know … I love you."

Her reaction was cut off by the doors to the back of the van flying open, and Danny and Parker sticking their heads in.

"Oh, he looks terrible," Parker assessed before disappearing in a flash.

Danny hauled himself into the back of the van, knee brace and all, and slammed the door shut behind him just as Parker revved the engine.

The only way I knew the van was moving was by tracking the subtle sway of Danny and Edith's bodies above me. Danny wouldn't look at me. I guessed he was afraid of the fear I'd see in his face, and he wanted to project strength. Edith had turned away from me too. Dying confessions of love weren't usually my thing, but in that moment, it felt like the right thing to do.

The jostle of bodies in and out of my dimming field of vision told me the van had stopped moving, and my ears picked up on the sound of footsteps on the ground outside. Light flooded my retinas and a tall figure loomed.

Harrison.

"What the hell happened?" His words rang painfully in my ears.

I tried to sit up, to speak, to do anything at all, but my body refused to respond. The nerve agent was coursing through my veins now, and doing its best to keep me down, and shut off every one of my bodily functions until I died under the weight of my own body. The fact I'd also been electrocuted didn't help matters.

"A vampire crew attacked us," Edith answered.

"Help now, questions later," Danny snapped, as he tried to drag my unresponsive body out of the van.

Edith was in my field of vision again, and her expression was hard to read. Maybe that had more to do with the dimming grey haze cast over everything around me. Whether she carried me inside or had help, I'll never know.

The interior of the base flashed by at inhuman speeds, and I assumed Edith had borne my weight. The numbness had given way to an icy chill as my body's systems continued to shut down.

As the world faded in and out of focus around me, I had enough sensation left to tell I'd hit a gurney. Voices flooded what was left of my hearing, but I couldn't pick out the individual words, let alone attribute them to individual speakers.

Stay awake.

The command was almost too much for my brain to follow. But, by sheer determination, I kept blinking, letting the lights above me filter in and out of the haze that was overshadowing everything.

"Hang in there, Paxton," someone said. *It could have been Harrison.*

Every breath was a struggle, but then, the weight on my chest lifted enough for me to breathe. Whatever had freed the burden, was also taking hold of the rest of me, trying to free me from the icy plunge, chasing it away with burning fire.

Pleasant at first, it transitioned into a white, fiery agony in seconds, and I may have screamed. I couldn't be sure, because it felt like I'd bitten through my tongue to keep silent.

"You're hurting him," Edith growled from somewhere.

"You need to let us work," an authoritative female voice said. I should have known that voice, but I couldn't place it.

Another low growl, this time promising an unspoken threat. A rustle of fabric was the only signal I had that Edith had left me with the med staff, doing all they could to beat back this poison. As I laid there, the burning receded to a strange tingling, and I pictured Edith in my mind's eye. Smiling, happy, and waiting for me. Danny stood at her side, beckoning me to join them.

They were what I had to live for now.

They would not take me out with some fucking nerve agent bullshit. I was going to fight and beat this thing. I refused to give Heartsong the satisfaction of taking me out by the coward's method. If he wanted me dead, he was going to have to try a lot harder and do the dirty work himself.

CHAPTER THIRTEEN

EDITH

I PACED BACK AND FORTH IN THE HALLWAY OF THE medical wing, trying not to think about Darren's precarious hold on life or what he said when he thought he was dying. Yet, no matter how hard I tried, I could not get the words *I love you* out of my mind. Did he mean it or was it just something he felt I wanted to hear? Articulating his feelings was not something Darren cared for. Feelings equaled weakness, and he made a point to never be seen as weak. The way he went out of his way to not be "sappy", amused me. I assumed any mention of "love" would be forever implied but never said. This was unexpected. Appreciated, yes, but unexpected. Why would he tell me such a sappy thing? *Maybe he meant it*, a voice whispered in the back of my mind. *Maybe he meant it.*

"Impossible," I said out loud.

"What is?" Dan asked.

I startled, forgetting I was not alone in the hallway. "Something Darren said to me before you and Parker arrived was peculiar that's all. I'm sure I'm overthinking it."

Dan rubbed his knee and leaned back against the wall. The overhead fluorescent lights of the medical wing were garish—reminding me of the sunlight we rarely saw because of battle tactics. In the dark, you were more likely to get bitten, which any Hunter worth their training would avoid. In the light, the clan used weapons to make up for their strength not being at full capacity.

"I should have insisted we come straight home when Darren found me this morning," I rambled. "I should have known the clan would fight dirty. Now he could … Now he could *die* because of me."

"It's not your fault," Dan said. "Don't worry. He's going to be alright."

I swiveled towards him. "You don't know that, Dan. None of us know that."

"You're right. We don't." Dan tried so valiantly to hold on to his stoic soldier expression, but it crumbled in an instant like a sandcastle hit by a wave. "I just … I need him to be okay, so I'm okay, you know? Darren is all I have left."

I realized in that instant how young Dan truly was. He was a teenager, but not an eternal teenager like Parker, Angel, or

Hope. He did not have their life experience that belied their physical age. He was a living, breathing almost eighteen-year-old boy who had experienced more heartache in his brief life, than most saw in their long afterlife.

"Darren is not all you have," I assured him. "You have myself, the girls, and Parker. I promise you, we are your family, Dan." I hugged him because that was what mothers do when one of their own was hurting. Dan stiffened before relaxing into my embrace. We hugged each other in the hallway, united by our love of Darren and our worry for his health. Dan pulled away first.

"Thanks," he murmured, cheeks flushed in embarrassment, "You don't know how much I needed that."

"As did I." I gave his hand one last squeeze before letting go. "Promise me you'll stay with Darren and find me the second he is allowed non-family visitors. Please?"

Dan frowned. "Why? Where will you be?"

"I need to speak with Parker," I said. "He can help me with something important. I believe the key to turning the tide in our war with the clan may be hidden within my memories." I wrung my hands in front of me, my new plan still barely half formed. It was a long shot, but one I needed to make for the good of humanity. "Parker studied psychology. Mr. Heartsong told me to search my suppressed memories from the time I was last with the clan. I am sure there are … unpleasant … moments hidden there, but I believe I may have overheard some of his battle plans too. Perhaps I even participated in their formation. Mr. Heartsong wished to taunt me when he told me to search for the 'truth', but I intend to make sure he can never harm me or anyone I care about ever again. Uncovering what's hidden in my mind is the best way to do that. Parker can help."

"What do you mean by unpleasant?" Dan asked.

I shook my head. "What I remember is hazy. I'm unsure if it is even real or not. Perhaps it is another false memory. He tried planting more than one of those during my return to the clan. If it is real, I—" I stopped short and shook my head again. I could feel Mr. Heartsong's hands on my shoulders, my arms, and lower, as surely as if he was standing in front of me now. I did not want to remember. I did not want to confirm my worst fears, but I needed to. If it helped us learn even a fraction of his plan, I needed to. "What he may have done—" I stopped again, pushing down the half-memories trying to fight their way to the surface. "Never mind. If I say it out loud, it makes it real. It makes it true. I will know the full truth of my missing days soon enough if Parker agrees to help."

"Are you sure you're okay?" Dan asked. "It feels like you're going into battle without really knowing what you're up against." He was silent a moment before adding, "If you're looking for Parker, check his room first. The training room and rec room kind of creep him out."

I nodded thanks before turning to leave. A final thought made me pause and look over my shoulder. "Oh, and Dan … Tell Darren I do not hold him to anything he said when he thought he was dying. He'll know what I mean."

CHAPTER FOURTEEN

DARREN

THE WORLD CAME BACK SLOWLY. JUST INDISTINguishable sounds at first. Then, my brain finally made sense of the repetitive beeping of the medical equipment hooked up to my body, tracking blood pressure, heart rate, oxygen. The thought of opening my eyes was too exhausting and so I laid there, just listening to sounds around me.

Something shifted off to my left, and it seemed like it took forever to turn my head towards the sound. I wanted to know what was going on. I was pretty sure I wasn't dead, and I'd like to know how I'd managed that. Plus, there was the matter of that little confession to Edith in the back of the truck. *That really happened, right?*

Not willing to give in to the pull of sleep, that a part of me knew was necessary for my recovery, I forced my eyes open, and took in the stark walls of the hospital room. The machines were to my right, beeping away. There were a few with little green lights. I assumed as long as they stayed green, the doctors would leave me alone. It was a struggle, but as I turned my head, I saw Sam sitting at my bedside.

"What are you doing here?" My throat was scratchy from lack of use and probably some aftereffects of the fucking nerve agent.

"Someone had to monitor you until you woke up," she said with a shrug. "And I may have promised your brother I'd come get him when you woke up. You've been out for nearly twelve hours."

Part of me believed her words, but there was also little that would keep Danny from me. Physical injury, death, or Harrison's orders. "Harrison wants a report, doesn't he?" I sighed.

She smirked. "What do you think?"

"I think I nearly fucking died. He can take his report and shove it up his ass."

She mimed taking down notes. "You want me to put that right at the top of my report?"

I'd flip her off, but I didn't have full control of my fingers yet. They tingled and twitched when I tried to move them. That was a good sign, at least. I wiggled my toes too. "We were just trying to do something normal, and a bunch of Heart-song's lackeys hit the diner. Guess they were making up for their decreased strength by playing dirty. Sadistic fuckers."

"They really must have caught you off guard for them to hit you with that toxin."

I didn't have a witty quip for that. So, I just laid there as that tingling that had started in my fingers and toes spread through the rest of my body. I grit my teeth as the feeling intensified and the heart rate monitor started blaring an alarm.

Footfalls outside the room thundered in our direction and the door burst open. A white-coat clad doctor I'd seen around base but couldn't remember what his name was, was at my side in seconds.

"What happened?" The doctor directed the question at Sam.

"I don't know. One minute he was talking, and then this," she answered, waving a hand at me as I tried and failed to not writhe in pain.

"It burns," I ground out.

"Give him another injection," the doctor barked.

I couldn't form the words to ask what sort of injection they were giving me or even if I wanted it. If it was going to make the agony stop, I'd take anything. A sharp prick to my left elbow told me they'd administered the injection.

The burning subsided, but so too did my ability to stay conscious.

The next time I woke up, the room was dark. My body didn't feel as stiff and I could move more easily. I rolled onto my side to find Danny slumped in the chair Sam had occupied.

He had stretched his injured knee out in front of him, supported by the knee brace.

"Danny?" I called.

He startled awake and looked at me, wiping the sleep from his eyes. "You're not dead," he said matter-of-factly.

"You think I'd go out that easy? Come on. A fire couldn't take me out. Some nerve shit won't put me out of commission for long." Hoping the bit of bravado would convince him I didn't feel like such utter garbage.

"You scared me," he whispered, not looking at me.

"Didn't mean to." I'd almost expected Edith to be there, hovering like a guardian angel over my bed. "Where's everyone else?"

"Still only family allowed," Danny answered.

"But Sam ..." I trailed off.

"Harrison can throw his weight around when he wants to. He wanted to know what happened, and he wasn't going to wait."

"Dude needs to learn some boundaries," I sighed. If he'd heard those words come out of my mouth, he'd have punched me.

"Edith was out there earlier, though," Danny offered, gesturing vaguely towards the door.

"Oh. Right."

"She told me to tell you she doesn't hold you to anything you said while you were dying. Whatever that means?"

I would have given anything to bury my face under the blankets, to hide the flush of embarrassment that washed over me. But all I could do was lay there, looking stupid in front of my little brother. "You know how it is, the poison takes hold and you're just not making sense," I rambled.

"What did you say to her?" He leaned forward and whispered, "Did you propose or something?"

"God, no," I scoffed. "I don't really remember much, but I'd remember that," I lied.

"You're lying, Darren. I'm not stupid. What did you tell her?"

I hated he could call me on my bullshit so easily. There'd been a time when he'd been younger, and I could tell him anything and he'd have believed it. That included promising that we'd hunt down the sons of bitches who murdered our parents and get justice. I still intended to make that promise a reality. "It's none of your business."

"It was something sappy, wasn't it? Man, you really must have thought you weren't going to make it if you got sappy."

"I can have feelings," I grumbled.

"Yeah, anger and horniness."

"Get out of here. I need my beauty rest," I said and made a shooing motion towards the door.

He hoisted himself up and walked to the door. Before he could get his hand on the knob, I added, "If you see Edith, tell her I'm not taking it back."

"I'm not your damn messenger service, you dick." I could hear the smile in his voice as he opened the door and disappeared, leaving me to submerge into unconsciousness again, dreaming of her face and the feeling of her body next to mine beneath the blankets.

CHAPTER FIFTEEN

EDITH

PARKER GRABBED HIS PHONE AS SOON AS THE message alert sounded and checked his screen. "It's from Dan," he said before glancing up at me. "Darren's awake, and, well, as Dan says, 'acting like typical Darren.'"

My anxiety, which had been at eleven out of ten since the diner ambush, relaxed slightly and I allowed myself to smile. "Did he say anything else?"

Parker checked his phone again. "Something about Darren not taking back whatever he said to you. You'd know more about it than I would."

I laughed. "Also, typical Darren. No apologies for any words—good or bad—that come out of his mouth."

"Which were these, good or bad?" Parker set down his phone, though I could tell he was itching to relay to Dan whatever I told him.

I thought for a moment. Which was it? I should consider being told "I love you" from my boyfriend a good thing. Though the weight of those words in our current situation made the sentiment tip a little to the bad side. Love made you do wonderful yet foolhardy things. Darren was reckless enough with his own safety. I did not need him to be overly so, in an unspoken mission to protect me. I could protect myself. But could I protect my loved ones?

"Edith?" Parker prodded.

I shook my head, clearing away the useless, circular thoughts. "I'm sorry. I get lost in my own mind sometimes." I forced a smile, realizing I had not answered his first question, nor did I intend to. "Now, where were we?"

"Darren being Darren, and you wanting to try again to access your lost memories." To his credit, Parker did not push me to disclose more than I was comfortable with. "I know our first session wasn't exactly successful, but that doesn't mean today's won't be. I'm willing to try if you are."

When I first came to Parker to use his psychology training to uncover my missing memories, we turned my room at the base into a makeshift, distraction free workspace. I felt comfortable here and trusted Parker. Both were keys to our success.

I tucked my skirt around my legs as I settled into a more comfortable position on the bed. Parker sat in the desk chair, a psychology textbook open across his lap. "Why did you become interested in psychology?" I asked, stalling for time. I was half-hesitant to try the process again if we were to be met with yet another failure. I could not help our side of the war if I could not remember what Mr. Heartsong planned.

"At first, I wanted to figure out why I was different," Parker said. "I thought maybe if I found out why my mind and impulses were how they were, I could fix them." He shrugged. "Then it became less a mission to fix something and more to help others. You can't fix something that isn't broken, and I'm not broken. I never was. It just took me too long to fully acknowledge that."

"I'm proud of you for doing so now."

Color darkened his pale cheeks. "Thanks. That's a very mom-thing to say. My own mom sent me to a conversion camp and shock treatment, where I learned to give the answers people wanted to hear instead of the truth. I would have said anything to get out of there." He gestured vaguely around the room, caught in his own memories. "I survived, which is all I can really say for myself. I'm not sure I've really lived that much until now."

"The Paxton brothers can be persuasive when they want to be," I agreed. "We are both living thanks to their influence."

Parker looked as if he wished to say more before he decided against it. He flipped a few pages of his book until he found the section he was looking for. "I think we should try visualization today. It's a form of hypnosis that could open your lost memories. All you have to do is get comfortable, close your eyes, and listen to the sound of my voice."

I adjusted the pillows behind my back and closed my eyes. Parker began speaking in a low, soothing voice. He led me through several visualization scenes, which relaxed my mind and body. Memories appeared, vying for attention. Daniel. Teaching. The First World War. I pushed them aside, looking for what I needed—what we all needed—in order to put an end to our current war.

The memory at first was hazy, but I held on until it solidified. I dropped myself down into the memory at Parker's suggestion. It felt as if I was there again, reliving it, but I also held onto enough of a detachment that I knew nothing I saw, or heard, or felt there, could hurt me. I was safe and able to return to the present when necessary.

"Tell me what you see," Parker requested, his voice still holding that soft, coaxing quality. "Are you alone?"

"I'm never alone," I said, surprised at the sound of my own voice. It was as if my subconscious was having a conversation with Parker. "He is always with me. Daytime. Nighttime. I'm never alone."

"Who is he?" Parker asked.

"Mr. Heartsong," I answered. "Though he says to call him Percival, but that's not his name either. Not his proper name. His proper name is *Sani*. It means 'old one.' He has seen so much. I like *Sani,* but he says never to call him that."

"Why not?"

"I don't know," I said. "He gave it up when he turned. He gave up his old life completely."

"Is he with you now?"

"He's always with me," I repeated. "Day and night. I told you that."

"Where are you now?" Parker asked.

"In his office at the mansion. He has a map spread across his desk. There are marks on it. He calls them his battle lines."

"Do you recognize the locations?"

"They're all around the city," I replied. "There are numbers underneath them. They might be dates."

"Dates of attack?" Parker asked. "Dates of battles?"

I felt myself shrug. "Dates relating to the battle lines. He won't tell me more. That's why he's with me day and night ... but mostly at night."

"Is there anything else you need to tell us about this memory?"

I paused as flashes of memory fought to be seen. Mr. Heartsong kissing me. Him climbing into my bed. Him fondling my breasts while I pretended to sleep. His fingers moved lower until ... Were these real or imaginary memories? I cringed and pushed them all down as far as they would go. "No. There is nothing else to tell you."

Parker led me through the reverse of the initial visualization exercise until I was firmly in the present and aware of my surroundings. Without a word, I stood and pulled open the desk drawer nearest Parker until I found paper and a pen. I wrote everything I remembered from the map and battle lines. I left out what else I saw of 'at night.' When I was finished, I held out the crude map to Parker.

"We need to show this to Harrison. Now."

CHAPTER SIXTEEN

DARREN

WHEN I WOKE UP, THE SKY OUTSIDE HAD DARKened past twilight and into nighttime. *Had I really slept another day away?* Time seemed too fuzzy, and I didn't like not knowing how long I'd been stuck in bed for. I'd never been the best patient, and I'd be damned if I'd let Heartsong's dirty methods keep me on bed rest forever.

A soft knock at the door drew my attention, and I sat up, trying to smooth down my hair on the off-chance Edith had come to check on me. Without waiting for me to give the okay to enter, the door flung inward, and Harrison marched in, trailed by Parker, Edith, and Dan.

"Good, you're awake," Harrison barked.

"Thanks for the concern," I muttered.

"Well, if you hadn't been off on a date, we wouldn't be here."

"So now you're judging my decisions to eat breakfast?"

Edith hovered on the periphery, staying well out of Harrison's field of vision, but not approaching me either. Had Danny not conveyed my message? Or was she too freaked out by it to acknowledge me?

"Neither Darren nor Edith asked to be attacked and, if they hadn't been there, dozens of civilians could have died," Parker interrupted.

I stared at him in his sweater vest and button-down shirt. He still looked like a nerd to me, but maybe that's what drew my brother to him. The look made him appear smart. But he'd never spoken to Harrison like that before.

"And, we have information we wouldn't have had otherwise," Parker continued, and held up a piece of paper with handwriting scrawled across it.

Harrison snatched it from his fingers and studied whatever was transcribed there. "Do we know what these mean?"

"I am afraid not. But they could be important. And they appear to be dates not yet passed," Edith offered softly.

Harrison rubbed the stubble on his jawline, considering the information. "And where did you say you saw this?"

If it was possible for Edith to lose what little color remained in her cheeks, it vanished right then. "I recalled more details of my brief return to the clan. I memorized some of this information, but I do not believe he confided in me what he planned to do on these dates or at these locations."

"What are the chances he knows you remembered these details?" I kicked the blankets off.

"He told me to search my memories for the truth. I suspect he'd hoped I would recall other details, which I did not." The way her lips pressed into a firm line and the skin tightened around the corners of her eyes, I knew there was something else weighing on her.

"Then we should check them out," I said, and made a grab for the list, but Harrison danced out of my reach.

"Slow down, Paxton," he chided. "It seems to me there needs to be some reconfigurations before we make a move."

The room went silent as all eyes fell on him. Intellectually, I understood the words coming out of his mouth, but emotionally, I had no fucking clue what he was talking about. "Reconfigurations?"

"I'm changing up the field op teams," he decreed.

"That's bullshit," I spat.

"Commander's prerogative." He stepped up, so we were nose to nose and gave me a little shove in the chest.

Normally, that move wouldn't have done a thing to me. But in this still-weakened state, I staggered back. I could blame a whole host of things; lack of food, lingering effects of the taser or the toxin. But he had a damn point. I wasn't at my best right now and that meant on an operational level, I shouldn't be making decisions.

"So, who are the new teams going to be?" asked Danny. He did his best to stand at attention like a good soldier, even if his brace made it clunky.

Harrison gestured to Danny. "You're still on mission control, kid. Until medical clears you to go out without that brace, I'm not risking you in the field."

He turned to Edith next. "You'll be paired with Poin Dexter over here and Sam."

"His name is Parker," Danny ground out.

"And Paxton, you'll be with Caden. He keeps insisting he's deprogrammed. Time we tested that theory. And because we want to be sure we've got vampire representatives on these teams, you'll take the girls."

Every fiber of my being wanted to protest. He was sticking me with the two weakest fighters and a loose cannon. If he wanted these missions to go off the rails, that was the best way to ensure it.

"Do you really believe that is the best use of resources? Surely there could be other arrangements," Edith protested.

"My base, my orders," Harrison replied and marched towards the door, forcing Danny to do an awkward shuffle backwards to get out of his way.

"First date on this little cheat sheet of yours is in two days. Paxton, you better be back in fighting shape by then."

He left the room without giving me time to get one last verbal jab in. My body ached from being upright for even just a short time, but I refused to sit down and admit defeat. A shower and some food could cure a lot of ills. It would cure this one too.

"He wants us ready in two days, then we'll be ready," I announced to the three others in the room.

"I know I'm not one to talk but you look like shit, bro," Danny said.

"I'll be fine. I'm already feeling better." He fixed me with a disbelieving glare. "I swear. Look, I'm going to grab a shower and I'll meet you down in the kitchen. I'm starving. And unless my internal clock is completely fucked, today is Taco Tuesday."

Danny rolled his eyes but grabbed Parker's hand and dragged him from the room, leaving Edith and me alone. I did my best not to telegraph how worn out I was, but she waved her hands at me in a motherly way and without even touching me, she knocked me on my ass.

"You do not have to lie to me. I know you are not happy about being paired with the girls," she said matter-of-factly.

"It's not that," I began, but she held up her hand for silence. "I know they are not the strongest fighters, but they are dedicated to this cause and they will defend their family, and that includes you and Dan."

"I just need to know I can rely on them in the heat of the moment. That they'll follow my orders without question if the time comes."

"They will. They respect you. They recognize that you have the superior training, even if they possess the superior strength and agility."

"It's not just that. I need to know I can count on them to do what I tell them in the event Caden loses his shit and turns on us again. They can't react emotionally. If I tell them they need to neutralize him, they need to listen."

"I believe this is a conversation you should have with them." She twisted her hands into the fabric of her skirt. I could read her body language well enough by now to know she was keeping something from me.

"Look, I don't know if Danny told you," I started, and she nodded.

"Parker said you meant what you told me in the van."

"I did. And I do." It was my turn to knead my hands. "Look, Edith, I don't really do a lot of emotions. It's just not my thing. Not that I don't have emotions, contrary to Danny's assessment, but I just don't let them out."

"I was aware of that aspect of your personality, yes," she conceded.

"So saying what I did, it was kind of a big deal. And I don't expect you to say it back or anything. I just needed you to know, it wasn't because I thought I was dying or anything."

She nodded and gave me a shy smile. "I appreciate you not putting pressure on me to reciprocate." Her hands flew to her mouth. "I mean to say, that you are not expecting it in return right this instant. I do not give my heart away lightly and I fear it may be battered still from loss."

"Neither of us are perfect," I said as I reached for her. "I wish you'd tell me what's been keeping you up. What did he want you to remember?"

Her hand that had been reaching for mine retracted. "I think he wanted me to believe certain sentiments were shared when I returned to the clan. But I know now that they were falsehoods implanted in my memory by his glamour."

"You mean about not trusting me or the rest of the Hunters?"

"No." She averted her gaze, and her usually shallow breathing quickened. "I think … I think he may have …"

She didn't need to finish the sentence. I could fill in the perverted blanks for myself. I wanted to wrap my arms around her and vow vengeance for the horrors he'd inflicted on her, but I could see she didn't want to be touched. "I'm going to make that bastard pay for everything he's put us through."

She took a few steadying gasps of air and gestured to the still-open door. "You should get cleaned up. You seemed so eager for Taco Tuesday. It would be a shame to keep Dan waiting."

Chapter Seventeen

EDITH

I stepped into the hall and shut Darren's medical wing door behind me, wishing to give him a modicum of privacy in order to get dressed. I forced down the impulse to leave for the mess hall without him. That would be outside the realm of my normal behavior, and I needed to act normal. If I acted normal, I could pretend everything *was* normal, when, in reality, everything was falling apart.

I knew my repressed memories must have been missing for a reason. My mind ensured there were blanks, partially from Mr. Heartsong's doings, but also, I knew now, from my own inner sense of self preservation. There was no putting the lid back on that box. Once those missing pieces were out, they were out. I could not shield myself from them any longer. The thought made me sick. I leaned against the wall, closed my eyes, and took a deep, calming breath. I needed to push all that aside for now. The further I pushed those thoughts and images aside, the better. I could not let Mr. Heartsong destroy me from the inside out.

"Hey, you waited!" Darren slipped into the hall and shut the door behind him. He was wearing clean jeans and a tight black t-shirt that Dan must have brought from his regular room. A twinge of guilt raced through me at not being by Darren's side when he needed me most, but 'family only' meant just that. Dan managed fine without me.

I smiled, but it felt forced. "Of course I waited. Did you think I would not?"

Darren shrugged one shoulder and began walking towards the mess hall. At first, his steps were quick and normal, but, as the hallway seemed to stretch on, his steps turned shuffling and he leaned heavily against the wall. I looped my arm around his waist.

"Here. Lean on me."

"I'm fine," he gritted out. "I don't need help."

"Everyone needs help sometimes," I reasoned. "If it makes you feel better, I'll let go before we reach the mess hall."

"It doesn't, but thanks … I guess."

"Did anyone even officially discharge you, or did you make up their minds for them?" I asked as we shuffled along.

"Nothing else they can do." Darren's expression was pinched, his face pale, as he concentrated on putting one foot in front of the other. "Time in that bed is time I should train."

"You can allow yourself to heal," I said. "That is not a sign of weakness, Darren. No one is indestructible, no matter how much you wish to appear so."

"Says the chick with super strength," he grumbled.

"Says the chick who can also be taken out by a pen," I corrected. "Strength and speed will do me no favors unless I am faster *and* smarter than the enemy."

"Faster is not really in my wheelhouse right now." Darren stopped outside the mess hall. He leaned heavily against the wall, out of breath, as we drifted through the base.

I took a step away from him, knowing he would not want to be seen as needing help in front of the rest of the Hunters once we entered. "Then you will just have to be smarter until you are fully healed."

"What am I now?"

I crossed my arms over my chest. "You are one of the most reckless people I know." I raised a hand when Darren opened his mouth to protest. "Just hear me out, please. You are reckless and fearless, two qualities I very much love and admire in you, but those same qualities prevent you from admitting when you need help. We are a team, are we not? A family? You, me, the girls, Dan, Parker, and even Caden. We are a family. Families help each other. Let us help you, Darren."

"I don't need help, Edith."

I took a step back, unable to mask the hurt that flashed across my face. "As I said, everyone needs help sometimes. Even you."

Darren muttered "I'm an asshole" under his breath before pulling me into a tight embrace. I stiffened slightly before relaxing against the safety and comfort of his body. I closed my eyes and pretended, for just a moment, that it was just him and me. No war. No injury. No haunting memories of a time I wish I could forget. Just us.

"I'm sorry," Darren murmured as he smoothed my hair with his calming fingers. "I'm not used to needing anyone. I've always been the strong one. I don't know what to do when that's all fucked up."

"Trust us," I said. "Trust *me*."

"I'll try my best." He kissed the top of my head. "You know you can trust me too, right?"

I wanted to ask, "*with what?*", worried that he would go digging for information I was not yet willing to share. Instead of questioning his intentions, though, I just nodded yes, and stepped out of his embrace.

"Of course." I attempted a weak smile. "We should get inside. Taco Tuesday waits for no man."

Darren grinned and stood up straighter, looking healthier and more like himself than he had in days. "Damn right. After that, I plan to sleep in my own bed." He winked. "Sleeping optional, of course."

I smiled—genuinely this time—buoyed by his good mood. "How much healing do you think you accomplished in two days?"

"Only one way to find out."

I tip-toed to kiss him. "You're incorrigible."

Darren rested his arms low and loose around my waist. “I’ve been called worse. Sometimes by you, but mostly by everyone else. I can take it.”

“You should at least offer to buy a girl dinner before jumping right into ‘sleeping optional,’” I teased.

His eyes widened in feigned shock. “What do you call Taco Tuesday if not the best dinner night of the entire week?”

I made a show out of considering my non-options. “I’ll take it. On one condition.”

Darren raised an eyebrow. “And what’s that?”

I leaned in to kiss him again. “You tell the girls they’re on your team now.”

CHAPTER EIGHTEEN

DARREN

I resented the bounce in Edith's step as she pushed through the door to the mess hall. I didn't agree with Harrison's assessment that the teams needed to be switched up, and I also didn't appreciate having to be the glorified fucking babysitter. For all his nerdiness, Parker at least had some skills. I straightened and followed Edith into the room. All eyes fell on me as I moved to stand in line, picking up a plate.

"Good to see you up," Sam said, as she looped around the other side of the buffet-style layout.

"You didn't think they'd keep me sidelined for long, did you?" I quipped, as I grabbed a mix of hard and soft taco shells, filling them high with beef.

"I heard you ducked out of medical against doctor's orders," she teased.

"Like you wouldn't have done the same damn thing."

"Oh, you know I wanted out of the white-coat quarantine as soon as humanly possible, but I also know that I'm not a doctor and sometimes we have to listen to our bodies, because they're better at telling us what we need more than our brains."

"Well, mine is telling me to eat these tacos with extreme prejudice and get back out in the field where I belong," I replied, and stalked off to the table Danny and the others had claimed in the corner. It was one of the few large circular tables in the room.

"I was thinking you'd changed your mind or passed out again," Danny jabbed, as I slid into the seat beside Edith.

I glanced around the table. Maybe it was because I'd eaten little in days, but the slight metallic scent of blood that the vampires mixed in with their food stood out to me like a neon signpost proclaiming their difference from the rest of us. I took a slow inhale through my nose and blew it out before picking up a taco.

"I told you, I wouldn't miss Taco Tuesday," I said, around a mouthful of food, earning me a few disgusted looks from the rest of the table.

"Dude, that's gross," Danny said, with a laugh.

I shook my head and focused on the food. The lack of food in my system became clear when my stomach gave an audible and angry gurgle after the fifth taco. I pushed the plate away and sucked in air as discreetly as possible. Which, I realized, was a futile task when surrounded by four vampires who had preternaturally enhanced senses.

"Mama E, how come everyone's been all excited this afternoon?" Hope asked, leaning her head against Edith's shoulder.

I tried to not think about how her body language screamed her youth and inexperience. Edith had sheltered them for so long, even with months of training, they were still too reticent to get their hands dirty or get up close and personal in a fight.

"Given that it is Hunter business, I think Darren ought to fill us all in," Edith said, giving me a pointed look.

I wasn't getting out of breaking the news. "We got some new intel on Heartsong's plans. Some potential strongholds around the city. We're being assigned locations to hit. The goal is to dismantle whatever we find."

"You mean take out other vampires," Angel breathed.

"Probably." I replied. It came out sounding cold, but it was the truth. They'd lived through a war before. Edith had saved them from it when they were children. I didn't get why they didn't understand that's what we faced now.

"Why can't they all understand we should be able to live together?" she sighed.

"Because Heartsong has brainwashed them into believing that his way is right. That vampires are superior to humanity. Because he's a fucking cult leader, and they're always far too charismatic for their own good," I snapped.

She flinched back at my words. I looked over at Edith, expecting her to give me a disapproving look for lashing out at her kids, but she just sat there patiently, one eyebrow slightly raised.

"Anyway, Harrison has decided in his infinite wisdom, that there needs to be some changes."

"What sort of changes?" Caden had been silent, picking at his food with his seat leaning against the wall. It was the farthest he could get from other people while still being in the group.

"A reorganization of resources," I said as diplomatically as possible.

"Meaning he's benching people," Caden sighed.

"On the contrary. You've been telling us for weeks you're ready. Well, you get to prove it. I'll be monitoring you though. And you know that if you step so much as a centimeter out of line, I'm going to nail your ass."

The color drained from his cheeks. "Got it."

"Are we with Dan?" Hope asked.

My brother shook his head. "I'm still grounded." He patted his knee brace. "Believe me, I wish I was out there with you guys, but the doctors still won't clear me."

"You're with me. Both of you," I said as quickly as possible, gesturing to her and her sister.

"What?" They yelped in unison.

"You heard me." I pushed away from the table. "I won't go easy on you. And I expect you both to pull your weight. And don't argue. If I give you an order, you follow it." I gestured for them to stand up. "Come on."

"Where are we going?"

"To train. We've got a few hours, if that, before we need to be in the field and I'm not satisfied you two are ready." I pointed to Caden. "You're coming too."

I caught the girls giving Edith a plaintive look, but she shooed them off to follow me. I wasn't going to be their damn babysitter. But I wasn't going in blind, either. I led them down to the training room, ready to drill them until we worked as a flawless unit … or died trying.

CHAPTER NINETEEN

EDITH

"AND THEN THERE WERE THREE." DAN TOOK A large bite of his hard-shell taco and stared at me as if I should have all the answers on what our next move was. "Should we tag along with D, C, and the girls or—?"

"As much as I would love to follow, unfortunately, the rationale for Harrison's decision is so we *aren't* always together," I said. "Besides, we have our own mission to contend with."

Parker perked up, eyes bright at doing something, just the three of us, versus being overshadowed by Darren's particularly gruff brand of leadership. "But Dan's not allowed out in the field yet."

"Dan's not allowed to fight in the field, but that doesn't mean he cannot run operations from the back of the van." I leaned across the table and patted the top of Dan's hand in a maternal fashion. "I realize how difficult it must be to stay behind while those you love rush off to danger. You're the only trained Hunter out of the three of us. We'll need your skills close at hand. Are you up for that?"

"Absolutely. When do we start?"

"Right now, if you're able," I said.

Dan nodded and jammed the rest of his food in his mouth. He leveraged himself to his feet by pushing off from the back of his chair. He swung his mostly immobile leg with the cumbersome knee brace to the right towards the dirty dishes drop off location. Parker jumped to his feet as well and grabbed Dan's tray before he could. He held it out of range when Dan swiped for it.

"Park, I'm not a complete invalid!" he whined. "Let me do simple stuff at least."

"Walking is not simple with all these tables and chairs scattered around the mess hall." Parker stubbornly held the tray out of Dan's reach. "Go get ready. Edith and I can handle the dishes."

"We'll meet you at the van in twenty minutes," I promised, hoping I'd given him—and us—enough time to return to our rooms, change into tactical gear, and meet up at the van. "Parker, you're driving, but be prepared for a fight just in case. We don't know what the meaning of these dates and locations are, but we are going to find out."

"I'm on it," he promised.

Dan crossed his arms over his chest and opened his mouth to protest before thinking better of it. He sighed and pivoted his injured leg towards the door. Beyond that leads to the dorms. I watched him limp away. His speed was improving, but his agility was next to nothing thanks to the heavy knee brace that extended above and below the injury to stabilize his entire leg. I hoped I was making the right decision by taking him along, instead of leaving him safely behind a computer monitor. Darren would never forgive me if anything happened to him. I would never forgive myself.

Parker cut the van's headlights and turned off the ignition. He turned toward me. "Are you sure this is the place?"

I double checked the sheet of paper I brought along with all the dates, times, and coordinates I observed on Mr. Heartsong's map. The date and time were correct, but the location surprised me. I craned my neck to get a closer look at the bright neon sign above the fairly nondescript windowless brick building. "What is, *The Blood Bag*?"

"It's a vampire night club." Parker shrugged when I shot him a, *and how would you know that?* look. "What? You've never heard of The Blood Bag? All the young vamps hang there."

"Since when?" Dan called from the back. "Cause if there's a place where you could pick off a ton of vamps without trying, the Hunters would know about it. This place should've been a burning pile of rubble years ago, if what you say is true, not a vampire discotech nest."

"I don't say it's true, I know it's true." Parker unhooked his seatbelt and climbed over the seat into the back of the van. I followed. "You, out of everyone, should know your intel is only as good as your field agents," he added. "*Because* you could easily dust members of multiple clans, that's why no one broadcasts the location of The Blood Bag. Think of it like a secret society."

"For teen vamps?" Dan scoffed.

"For anyone wanting to forget, for one night, that Hunters could stake them at any moment," Parker shot back. "Look, I don't know why this location holds any significance to Mr. Heartsong's plans, but I'll go in and see what I can find out." He stuck his earpiece in his right ear before swinging the van's back doors open and hopping down. "Keep your audio on. I'll report back when I can."

"Should I come with you?" I asked. "There is safety in numbers."

"And leave Dan unprotected?" Parker shook his head, ignoring Dan's dark scowl at the implication he could not protect himself if it came to a fight. "No. This is a solo intel mission."

"At least keep your infrared sensor on so we know how many vamps we're potentially dealing with," asked Dan .

Parker gave a slight salute in parting before striding up to the front door of The Blood Bag and knocked three times. A door panel slid open to determine the situation. Parker pointed at himself as if to say 'it's me' before the gatekeeper swung open the entire door to let him inside.

"So, do you think it's like a gay bar or something?" Dan asked once Parker disappeared inside. "I mean, how much do I really know about what he's been up to before we got together? He could be some teen vampire gigolo for all I know."

"We have no reason to believe this place is anything more than how Parker described it," I tried to smooth over his prominent jealousy, but he still only knew what Parker would tell him, which was, usually, not much. I can't say I blamed Dan. I felt the same pang of jealousy when one of Darren's many ex-girlfriends appeared before me. It made me question everything I thought I knew about how I fit into his life, just as Dan was perhaps questioning how he fit into Parker's.

"I've got work to do," Dan grumbled, as he slid his laptop closer and pulled on his headset. "Park, can you hear me?"

"Roger," Parker's voice crackled over both our earpieces. "Are you getting my infrared feed?"

Dan punched a couple of keys on his laptop to pull up a choppy, live video feed of the interior of the club. The heat readout showed the dance floor crowded with less-than-warm bodies. "Fifty," Dan murmured. "Maybe upwards to sixty or seventy. What is Heartsong playing at?"

"Perhaps it is a recruitment effort and not anything anti-human," I suggested.

"That doesn't make me feel any better."

"I'll scope it out, see what I can find," Parker said.

His video feed became jumpy as he moved around the large single room of the club. Nothing appeared out of place or even remotely suspicious. The Blood Bag, looked, for all intents and purposes, to be exactly what Parker said it was—a place for young vampires to dance and forget their worries.

Dan cut the microphone to his feed before asking, "So, how long do you think Park's been coming here? Did he, like, sneak out of the clan headquarters? Did he take the girls here? Why would he keep something like this a secret?"

I held my hands out, palms up. "I wish I could answer your questions and give you a modicum of peace, Dan, but I cannot. Our time with the clan was generally limited to recruitment weekends and holidays over these last five years. I'm sorry, I don't know what Parker does in his free time."

"Or who," Dan grumbled.

"I'm sorry," I repeated. "This is the part where I tell you you should trust him. Parker is kind and decent and caring. Don't push that away because of perceived secrets."

"Just like you're pushing Darren away?"

I frowned. "I am not pushing Darren away."

"I know he told you he loves you," Dan said. "So, what, you've been pretending like you didn't hear it this whole time since the diner incident?"

"He thought he was dying," I murmured. "People say unusual things when they think they may not get the chance again."

"Not Darren," Dan insisted. "Trust me, those words are like his kryptonite, Edith. He'd rather die than admit he cares about someone besides me. But he said them. To you. Now what are you going to do about it?"

"Nothing." I pushed the rear van doors open and climbed out into the deserted parking lot. I wanted—no, I needed—

to get away from Dan and his overly perceptive line of questioning. What he failed to realize was, every mortal I've loved, died. Why would I shackle Darren with such a fate? The more I hold back, the longer he lives.

"I'll check the perimeter," I volunteered before using a burst of vampire speed to race around the dark parking lot. Even if I could not outrun my relationship problems, it still felt good to run. It felt good to focus on something solid like my feet on the pavement instead of the muddle in my mind and heart. I stopped short during my second perimeter pass when I heard something.

"Edith remembers nothing." It was a voice I knew all too well, the words floating to my finely tuned ears through a half-open window. "I made sure of it."

"You can't glamour away the truth," someone replied. I recognized that voice too. It was Michael, one of Mr. Heartsong's key lackeys and the judge during Dan's sham trial at the last recruitment weekend. "It's always there, waiting. If she goes looking, our plan is toast."

"She won't go looking," Mr. Heartsong insisted. "Trust me." Plan? Did that mean there were more to the dates, times, and locations than just potential attacks? What else were they trying to do? I took an instinctive step towards the open window, wanting to learn more. Before I had a chance, Dan's frightened voice screamed in my ear:

"Edith! Parker! Get back now!"

I turned and sprinted back to the van. As I drew near, I saw the reason for Dan's terror. Two large vampires I didn't recognize from the Heartsong clan were dragging him out of the van by his braced leg. Dan swung his fists wildly, trying to fend off the surprise attack. The more he struggled, the more they laughed at his efforts.

"Lookee what we have here," the first sniggered, swaying slightly as if drunk. "A widdle human."

"A widdle hunter human," the second one said, similarly tipsy. "Do you know what we do to hunters?"

"We kill them!" the first laughed. "Time to make an example of you, widdle human. Don't worry. It won't hurt … much."

"Don't you dare touch him!" Parker howled, speeding to Dan's rescue. "You touch him, you die."

The drunk vampire thugs stopped their assault on Dan to assess this fresh development. "Get real kid. You're one of us."

"That doesn't mean I won't hurt you." Twin stakes flashed in Parker's hands. "Last warning. Touch him and die."

The thugs exchanged a look before both shrugged and ignored Parker. His sweater vest and khakis did not scream *intimidating*. Though, to be fair, I doubted my way of dressing would do much better.

"Go home, kid," the first vampire thug said. "You're up past your bedtime."

"Go to hell!" Parker lobbed a stake at the first thug. It bounced off his leather jacket and spiraled across the parking lot. I hurried to pick it up before anyone else thought to.

"Is that all you got?" the second thug taunted. He grabbed Dan by the shirt collar and pulled him roughly to his feet. He flashed his fangs before digging his teeth into Dan's neck. There was no request and no consent. That meant he wasn't planning on turning him. He was planning to kill him.

"Let him go!" I ran forward, the stake clutched in my hand. I spun and stabbed the thug closest to me, which wasn't the one sucking the life out of Dan. He gave a surprised grunt, looking down at the stake I'd lodged in his chest, before blood bubbled up from his mouth. He blinked at me, as if not fully comprehending what was going on, before he fell onto the stake, dead. There was no chance of getting my weapon back. Dan needed help now, before it was too late. "Parker!" I yelled. "Help!"

"On it!" he called before landing a blow to the back of the thug who was on Dan. When nothing happened, Parker yanked his stake out and aimed better. It distracted the thug long enough for Dan to elbow him in the gut and wrestle free. He tipped forward against the back of the van, leaving a blood-red handprint against the white paint. Parker continued to stab the thug until he was riddled with stake holes.

"Parker!" I said, first softly but then louder when he ignored me. "Parker! Parker, he's dead. You can stop now. You can stop."

"I told him not to touch Dan." Parker jerked his stake free before wiping a bloody hand across his face. "I told him, but he didn't listen. He didn't listen."

I placed a hand on either side of Parker's shoulders and leaned forward to make sure he paid attention to me, and not the surrounding carnage. "Parker, listen to me. Dan needs medical. I need you to drive. Can you do that?"

He nodded. "Yeah. Yeah, I can do that."

Parker helped me get Dan into the van and onto the mattress, before shutting the doors and hurrying around to the driver's side. I pulled out every gauze I could find in the first aid kit and pressed them against Dan's neck. He reached up and wrapped his blood fingers around my wrist.

"Edith? I don't want to die."

"You're going to be alright," I whispered. "I promise. You're going to be alright, Dan."

"I don't want to die," he repeated, voice faint.

"You won't." I smiled to cover up the fact I did not know if that was true or not. For the second time in three days, I prayed for the life of one of the Paxton brothers.

"Please be alright," I whispered. "Please be alright."

CHAPTER TWENTY

DARREN

I HIT THE RESET BUTTON ON THE TRAINING ROOM wall, and the figures returned to their upright positions. Caden, Angel, and Hope stood at the far end of the room, looking admittedly miserable. Caden bent double, hands pressed to his knees as he tried to catch his breath. He'd at least been trying to execute what I'd been asking for. The girls just glared at me, like I was the cruelest person in the world.

"Run it again," I said, waving for them to come back to the start.

"We've done this like ten times already," Caden huffed.

"And you still aren't working together. So, run it again,"

"Caden's tired," whined Angel.

"We're all tired. Do you think the enemy is going to give two shits if you didn't get your beauty sleep?"

"I'm fine, Angel," Caden said and jogged back towards me.

"You don't have to be so mean," sniped Hope.

"Look, I didn't ask for this team. But we're going to make the best of it. And until I'm confident you can execute a plan without giving yourselves away, we're going to drill."

I didn't enjoy being hard on them. But they were still so inexperienced. Maybe there was a reason few children were turned. No matter if their bodies matured into adulthood, their mentality would always be stuck.

"I think maybe the problem is, we aren't communicating," Caden offered.

"You need to anticipate where the others are going to be. You've got heightened reflexes. Use them," I addressed the girls.

They shared a glance and Hope chewed her lower lip. She looked on the verge of a meltdown, and I didn't have the time or energy to deal with whatever drama was coming. But I knew Edith wouldn't forgive me if I bruised one of her kids, even emotionally.

"What?" I gestured to her with the blunt end of a stake.

"What if we have to kill them?" Her words were barely above a whisper.

"There's no if in this equation," I said. "This is a war. Death is inevitable. You're going to have to take lives if you want to survive."

"We didn't sign up for a war," Caden said, stepping closer to the girls.

"Heartsong didn't give you a choice. Just one of the many reasons he's a vile son-of-a-bitch."

"We want to be brave for Mama E, but we don't want to fight," Hope reiterated.

"And you think I do?" I crossed my arms over my chest. I meant for it to look like I was being stern, but I just needed to give myself something physical to focus on, so the fatigue of just standing up didn't catch up to me.

"Well, yeah," Angel answered with a nod.

I wanted to snap at her, but I couldn't. Because she wasn't wrong. I'd trained half my life for this. It had become my mission to hunt down and eradicate the vampire species. Harrison had molded me into a model soldier and fighter. But it hadn't been the life I'd envisioned for myself. Or for Danny. I'd never stopped to realize that Harrison had taken a grieving child and turned him into a weapon. I'd been so blinded by anger and hate, I'd let him without question.

Edith had taken these girls from a terrible situation and gave them a chance at a normal life. Or as normal as she could manage, as a vampire. But she had never made them to fight.

"I get that you're scared. Every time we walk out those doors, there's a higher likelihood we aren't walking back in. I'm sure Edith would rather you sit at home, safe, and hidden from the carnage, but we don't have that luxury anymore."

"Do you get scared?" Angel asked, wrapping her hands around Caden's forearm.

"If you tell anyone I will flat-out deny it, but yeah. I get scared."

Her shoulders relaxed. "Let's try it one more time," she said to her sister and boyfriend.

I tossed the stake I'd been holding to Caden. He caught it in both of his and turned to the training course. "Hope, flank left, Angel, go right."

I watched as they spread out across the room. They were starting to move in lockstep. Caden's reflexes had gotten better. He avoided staking innocents, and as they neared their target, he caught Hope's eye and held up the stake a second, before he tossed it her way. In the blink of an eye, she'd caught the weapon and passed it to her sister, who slammed it hard into the practice dummy.

"Good," I said when they reached the end of the course.

Caden grinned. "Just needed better communication."

I didn't have time to give him an "atta-boy" before a set of footsteps thundered down the stairs. Sam flew into view. "You need to get to medical."

"I told the doctors I'm fine," I said, waving her off.

"It's Dan. He's hurt."

For a minute, time stopped as the words computed in my brain. It wasn't possible for Danny to be hurt. He was stuck behind a computer console to keep him safe. She had to be wrong. But she wouldn't make something like this up. We'd gotten past our drama. Which meant something had happened to Danny.

I pushed past her, racing up the stairs and slingshot myself down the hall and up the second set of stairs to the medical wing. I slammed open every door on the wing until I found the one where the doctors hovered around my brother's body. There were too many of them crowding him for me to see what was wrong. The bloody gauze pads hit the floor. They weren't bothering with his knee, which meant he was bleeding from somewhere higher up.

"What the fuck happened?" I demanded and stepped into the room.

A white-coated doctor spun, his hands covered in Danny's blood, and he gestured for me to go back the way I'd come. "We need to stop the bleeding and we don't need you trying to get in the way."

I shook my head until a nurse, who shouldn't have been able to push me around, gave me a solid shove and I staggered back into the hallway. She shut the door, and I heard the metallic click of a lock engaging. The adrenaline that had let me race up here ebbed more rapidly than it should have, and I slumped against the wall.

"Darren." Edith's voice roused me, and I turned to see her waiting at the far end of the hall.

"What happened?" My words carried less bite this time.

"There was an ambush," she replied, not meeting my gaze.

"What does that have to do with Danny? Why would an ambush affect him when he's running coms from here?"

"Because … he wasn't running them from here. He was in the back of the van."

"No. Harrison didn't okay that."

Her gaze lifted, so she was looking at a spot over my right shoulder. "He was the only trained Hunter on our team. I decided …"

"*You* decided? He isn't fit to be in the field," I snapped.

"I thought he would be safe in the van. But they were waiting. They took him and bit him. If Parker hadn't stopped them ..."

"You disobeyed a direct order." I ground out.

"And since when do you follow the rules so strictly?" she argued.

"When a superior gives it," I snapped back.

"You have never bucked authority? Not once?"

"Not with my brother's safety. You put him in harm's way. And now he's in there, fighting for his life. He's the only family I have left."

What little color she'd had in her face drained. "I thought we were your family."

Anger washed over me, warring with a nugget of guilt at my words. I couldn't be near her right now. I stomped away from her without a word, making it back to my room before the anger bubbled over and I slammed my fist into the wall. Plaster dust came away as I pulled my hand free. I'd probably broken a knuckle or two, but the pain didn't register. My body finally gave out, and I collapsed on the bed, my wounded hand clutched to my chest as I let the world fade to black.

CHAPTER TWENTY-ONE

EDITH

I SUNK TO THE GROUND AFTER DARREN DISAPPEARED. My heart told me to follow him, but my head knew I was the last person he wanted to see. No matter how much I pretended we were all one big, happy, extended family, he was right. Dan was the only blood relation he had left. And I had put him in jeopardy.

"Mama E? Is Dan going to be okay?"

I looked up to see Hope, Angel, Caden, and Parker clustered in the hall. Parker had changed out of his blood-stained clothes. The girls and Caden were dressed in black and looked fresh from a training workout. They were heading to the training room when Dan, Parker, and I left for the mission. Had so little time really passed since then? It felt like a lifetime ago.

"Mama E?" Angel prompted. "What happened to Dan?"

"They ambushed us," Parker answered for me. "Though I don't know if they really knew we were coming or were just looking for a fight and picked us." He wiped a shaking hand across his face, trying to hide the tears shimmering in his eyes. "They pulled Dan out of the van and … and bit him."

"Does that mean—?" Hope couldn't finish her sentence. There were rules all clans must follow. Turning someone against their will was one of them.

"They did not want to turn him," I said. "They wanted to kill him." I looked down at my own blood-stained hands, unsure if it was Dan's blood, the vampire thug's blood, or a mixture of both. "So much blood. Parker, you were very brave. Dan needed you, and you were there."

He shrugged off my praise. "I only did what they trained me to do. Dan would have done the same." He glanced around his circle of friends. "Dan would have done the same for any of us."

"Then what can we do for him?" Caden asked. "Does he need blood? Cause he can have mine. Or I can organize a blood drive. Whatever he needs, he'll get it."

"Why were you even out in the field, Mama E?" Angel asked. "What were you chasing?"

I pulled the sheet of dates and locations out of my pocket and climbed to my feet before passing it to her. "Answers to what all this means. In all the commotion, I forgot to tell you he was there. Mr. Heartsong was there. These dates and places mean something to him. If we find out what, there is a genuine possibility we can end this war, now."

Angel unfolded the paper. The girls and Caden crowded around while Parker crossed the hall to the door the medical staff ushered Dan through. He pressed his hands against the frosted glass, the hurried movements beyond the door told us nothing more of Dan's condition. Had they rushed him to surgery? Had he already received a blood transfusion? Would they tell us anything or wait for Darren before we knew the full extent of his injuries? I rubbed my throbbing temples. This night definitely did not go as planned. Nothing since this war started has gone as planned.

"These dates and place markers are battles," Caden announced, bringing me back from my thoughts. "There were a whole string of vampire losses towards the end of the Vampire-Human Civil War that caused them, to, well, lose. These dates all reference when vamps took an L in the war."

"Are you sure?" I wouldn't allow myself to hope for a break-through. Not yet, at least.

Caden nodded. "Positive. I'm the president of the Teen Vampire-Human Alliance, remember? You don't become the prez without honing up on vampire-human history. These are battles—more specifically, vampire losses —from the Civil War."

"So that means, what?" Angel asked. "That Mr. Heartsong wants a do over?"

"Not *wants* one, trying for one." Caden paced the hall, his face alight with ideas, as all the puzzle pieces fell into place. "What if he's hitting up all the old sites to say they won? To erase the stain of defeat or whatever he'd call it? We all know the dude is a petty douchebag. I can totally see him waiting for the big 150th anniversary of the war to start a new one. One he plans to win this time."

Of course. It all made complete sense now. If Mr. Heartsong had learned one thing in his long afterlife, it was the art of patience. He did nothing haphazardly. Every move had a meaning and purpose. Even if that meant waiting one-hundred-fifty years to right what he saw as an affront to vampire kind. Losing the Vampire-Human Civil War was the start of vampire subjugation. By reigniting the war, he hoped to gain what we had lost all those years ago—our basic civil rights. But he forgot there were other ways to achieve that goal.

Winning a war did not automatically mean vampire and human rights flip-flopped. It only meant bloodshed and more distrust between the groups. We needed to work with humans for a better future—not force it through fighting.

"Caden. Girls. Take this information to Harrison," I instructed. "Parker, wait here for word on Dan."

"What are you going to do, Mama E?" asked Hope.

"I am going to find Darren and tell him about our breakthrough." *After that, I am going to ask him to forgive me for putting Dan in harm's way,* I thought, as I opened my mouth to say more before thinking better of it. My regrets were not something I wished to share with the teens. They were mine and mine alone. Darren was the one who needed to hear "I'm sorry." I owed him that. I owed him a reason I was so hesitant to accept and reciprocate his "I love you."

"Go now," I urged the girls and Caden. "We will meet back here in an hour."

CHAPTER TWENTY-TWO

DARREN

THE THROBBING IN MY HAND STIRRED ME FROM my stupor. I rolled over and groaned as I landed on my injured knuckles. I looked down in confusion. I didn't remember getting into a fight recently. But every time I flexed my fingers, they ached.

"Shit," I swore and sat up, cradling my hand against my chest to minimize the throbbing.

I had just enough time to look around the room for something to wrap my hand in when there was a knock on the door.

Whoever was on the other side didn't bother to wait for me to answer. The door swung inward, it was Edith.

"What happened?" She was at my side in an instant, cupping my wrist between her fingers.

I looked around the room, spotting the hole in the drywall where my fist connected in anger. I knew I was supposed to be mad at her for dragging Danny into the field, but the way she looked at me, with such concern and fear, squashed any angry feelings.

"I lost a fight with the wall," I muttered and tried to shirk off her tender touch.

"You need medical attention."

"I'm fine."

"You are not fine. Do not make me drag you up there myself," she said, her tone more like a stern parent than a concerned girlfriend.

As I studied her profile, it reminded me just how much older she was. Her youthful appearance was such clever camouflage. "I shouldn't have yelled at you."

"Yes, you should have. Taking Dan into the field was a risk, and I knew that. I was foolish to believe that he would be safe in the van. And now he is fighting for his life because of me."

I winced as she probed my hand. "Well, I shouldn't have told you, you weren't family. That was cruel of me, and I'm sorry I was being such a douchebag."

She arched a dark brow in my direction. "Darren Paxton apologizing. This really is a new world."

"I'm trying this whole emotional growth thing. I don't know if it will stick, but I'm working on it."

"Let's get your hand looked at. And you can check on Dan."

I allowed her to help me stand, and we walked together to the medical wing. It was quiet as the sun crested the skyline outside. *Had tacos really only been a few hours ago? Had it been such a short time since I'd seen my brother laughing and happy with his friends?* I pushed those thoughts down, focusing on the pain in my hand, letting it ground me in the here and now.

"I do not expect your forgiveness for my mistake, but I hope that you might look at me again as someone you care for," Edith murmured, as we reached the far end of the medical wing.

"War is messy, Edith. I understand that. I just have a short fuse when it comes to Danny. I know he wants to be out there in the thick of it. Sometimes I look at him and all I can see is the little boy I dragged out of a burning building. I forget that he's basically an adult, capable of making his own decisions. I know he wouldn't have gone with you if he didn't think he could handle it."

She stayed quiet as we waited for a nurse to notice our presence. "He kept saying he did not want to die," she finally offered.

"I think that's the case with most of us. We go out into this crazy fucking world and we just hope we make it back in one piece."

Edith lapsed into silence again as a nurse spotted us, and I held up my battered hand. She rolled her eyes and gestured for us to step into one of the rooms down the hall. She shooed Edith away when I held up my good hand.

"She stays."

"Your call," the nurse sighed, and started poking at my hand. "I'd say you got lucky."

"Yeah?"

She wrapped my arm in a lead covering and shooed Edith out of range of the x-ray machine. It gave a metallic buzz as it took an image of my hand, putting it up on a screen on the wall. "Whatever hit you didn't break anything."

"Guess I should tell Harrison we need harder walls," I joked.

"I'll wrap it and ice it, but you'll be fine in a few days," the nurse assessed.

"What about my brother? When can I see him?"

"He's sleeping now. You can see him in a few hours."

That he was sleeping was a good sign. It meant they'd stopped the bleeding. The nurse grabbed my forearm and propped my elbow up on my knee. "Hold your hand like this until I get back. I'm going to need more gauze and medical tape."

She left the room, and Edith returned to my side. "It sounds like Dan is going to be okay."

I caught the relief as it loosened the tension in her shoulders. I had to admit my own anxiety lowered a few degrees too. "Why were you coming in before?"

"What do you mean?"

"You just kind of barged in. Not really your style, especially if we've … been arguing."

"I wouldn't classify what happened in the hallway as an argument, so much as you shouting at me. But, yes, I had a reason," Edith said. "Caden believes he has figured out the meaning behind the information I gleaned from Mr. Heartsong's map."

"And that would be what?"

"He is trying to reverse the vampire losses at key battles from the original Civil War."

"He's so ancient he probably lived them," I sighed.

"Yes, and I believe he has been waiting this long to right the wrongs." She produced the handwritten list again. "This date, in two days' time, is the final date. Which means it is the final battle that lost the vampires the war."

"So we take the fight to him. We crash his little party and kick his ass."

"We can't go alone. Nor can you and the girls."

"So, we convince Harrison that this needs to be an all-out assault on Heartsong's forces. Trust me, we pitch it like that, Harrison will agree in a heartbeat."

"When we met, you told me all the Hunters here had lost someone to vampires. Who did Harrison lose?" Edith asked.

"He was part of the National Guard. He lost his unit in a clash with some vamps."

"That makes so much sense," she murmured.

The nurse returned with gauze and tape and went about securing my hand. I didn't want to admit it, but the stabilization felt pretty damn good. "Keep it wrapped, Paxton. I mean it," she chided, before leaving again.

"Please promise me you won't go picking fights with walls again," Edith said, pressing her hands to my cheeks.

"I'll do my best." I gazed into her eyes and saw a wealth of emotions reflected. "Don't you love me?"

I didn't expect those words to come out of my mouth, and clearly neither did she. She stepped back, dropping her hands to her sides. "It is complicated."

“Not really. I mean, we all know I’m shit with expressing how I feel. As Danny said, I do angry and horny, and that’s about it. But, you’re different. You make me feel things I never thought I would again. I know we don’t always see eye to eye, but I thought that was part of our charm. I’ve never had someone call me out on my shit before.”

She toyed with the fabric of her skirt, keeping her eyes downcast. “I have been afraid to admit how I feel because … I thought it would keep you safe.”

“What does that mean?”

“Every person I have loved has died,” she whispered. “Daniel, my mother, friends I made during my time in the VHA. Inevitably, they die.”

“Because we’re human, and that’s what happens. We get old, we die,” I pointed out.

She shook her head. “Daniel was so young when he died.”

“War is a bitch. But you loving them didn’t make them die,” I told her. “Edith, I may get battered and bruised, but that’s what I signed up for. Long before I met you. Having you in my life has made me see what I have to fight for.” I reached out with my good hand and cupped her chin, lifting her face so our eyes met.

“You don’t think I’m worried that you’re going to go out there and end up with a stake in your chest? Of course I do. That doesn’t mean I love you any less or that I don’t want you to know how I feel. I want you to know it even more. So that, if one day, we don’t come back, we’ll go out knowing we made a difference. That we mattered.”

Pale blue tears trickled down her cheeks. "I never thought I would see the day when Darren Paxton, mighty Vampire Hunter, waxed poetic about his emotions."

"Yeah, well, drink it up now because it won't last for long."

"I do love you." She leaned forward and kissed me.

"Now that we've cleared that up, let's convince Harrison that we need to crash Heartsong's pity party."

CHAPTER TWENTY-THREE

EDITH

DARREN DID HIS BEST TO STRAIGHTEN UP AND look healthy and presentable when we reached Harrison's office. I was thankful I had seen fit to wash up in the communal ladies' room before going to Darren's. I don't like blood on my hands—especially Dan's.

Before we could knock, Hope, Angel, and Caden came pouring out of Harrison's office all in a jumble, talking at once.

"Mama E! Mama, you should have seen Caden in there!"

"He was *fabulous*!"

"Just doing my part. How's Dan?" Caden added when he saw Darren beside me.

"Sleeping." Darren's expression was pinched around his eyes and mouth, but he sounded normal and stayed upright. Thank God for small favors. "Better than the alternative."

"Totally," Hope agreed. "Let us know when he can have visitors!"

"Get some rest!" I called as they moved as a group down the hall towards the dorms. "And no boys in your room!"

"You are so old school, Mama E," Angel complained.

"But she didn't say Caden couldn't have *girls* in his room," Hope pointed out.

"Nice loophole." Angel high fived her sister before blowing me a kiss over her shoulder. "We'll be good, Mama E. Trust us."

"Those girls," I sighed, once they were out of sight.

"They're good kids," Darren said. "Annoying as all hell sometimes, but still good kids. They have you to thank for that."

"It is a slight backhanded compliment, but I will take it," I teased.

"Are you two planning to stand around in the hallway all day or come in and do something useful?" Harrison barked from inside his office.

We flinched as if he caught us doing something inappropriate out in the open.

"Well?" Harrison snapped. "I'm waiting."

My hand hovered near Darren's elbow as we entered Harrison's office, just in case his strength failed him, and he needed a little support. The stress of his own injury, and non-doctor approved shortened recovery time, followed by Dan's fight for life would be enough to crumble anyone else. Not Darren

Paxton, though. No, he stood at attention in front of his supervisor's desk as if nothing had changed in the previous handful of days. He was still the strong Hunter awaiting orders. Ready to do his duty. I admired his strength and tenacity. Very few would still be standing after all he had seen and experienced in his brief life.

"At ease." Harrison motioned at the vacant seats across from him. "The kids filled me in on the breakthrough. Now, what do you have?"

Darren sunk into a chair. I remained standing, hands resting on the back of his chair. If he needed physical support to stand, I could lend that without being overly obvious. "If Heartsong wants a fight, we give him a fight," Darren said. "And I'm not talking sending one or two teams. I'm talking about the entire base. Every Hunter needs to stream into his pity party and blow the whole thing sky-high." He cracked the knuckles on his good hand. "This is it. Little Bitch-Baby lost the first Civil War, and he's about to lose the second."

Harrison rubbed his chin, considering the plan. "A last push to stop the war before it drags on, or Heartsong overwhelms us with his newly turned vamp army. You've come up with worse ideas, Paxton."

"Worse?" he grimaced, his 'everything is alright' veneer started to crack. "This is epic, sir. Since when don't you want to win the war?"

"Our numbers are bound to take a hit. We may not recover from it." Harrison slid a map across the desk with a large circle around the coordinates of the final battle with the date three days hence scrawled next to it. "Location look familiar, Paxton?"

Darren squinted at the map. "My family's place?"

"And the date?" Harrison prompted.

The color drained from Darren's face. "The anniversary of the fire."

"Bingo." Harrison played with a lighter, flicking the flame on before extinguishing it and repeating, perhaps lost in his own thoughts of that night twelve years ago. "You always said Heartsong played the long game. Nothing is a coincidence with that bastard, is it?"

"No, sir, I don't believe so."

"Get some rest," Harrison dismissed us. "Lie low while you can. You'll need all the strength, know-how, and training you've got come Tuesday."

"Yes, sir," Darren said.

"Thank you, sir," I added, placing a steadying hand on Darren's forearm as he pushed himself out of the chair. "And sir? I know my apology means nothing afterwards, but I am sorry for what happened to your National Guard unit. I have always sided with peace, not bloodshed, between vampires and humans. Perhaps that puts me at a disadvantage with my kind, but it is the right thing to do, so I gladly do it. Mr. Heartsong is my sire, but you have my word I shall do everything in my power to stop him from hurting any more people."

He blinked, surprised at my candor. "Thanks, Dorset. Now get out of here too."

We both nodded before exiting Harrison's office, shutting the door behind us. I sighed. "What now?"

Darren wrapped an arm around my shoulders and pulled me to his side. "You heard the man. We gotta get some rest … or not rest. You know me. I'm shit with orders."

"You are still unwell," I reminded him. "Though I suppose some not-resting is in order." I tip-toed to kiss him. "The world may end in three days."

"I hear end of the world sex is better than make up sex," Darren joked … or, at least, I believe he was joking. I could never tell when he grinned at me like that if he was serious or not.

"Sleep." I swatted his non-injured hand that was creeping up my blouse. "Then we will talk about what to do, or not to do, in bed before the end of the world."

"Yes, ma'am." He kissed the top of my head before leading the way back to his—no, our—room.

CHAPTER TWENTY-FOUR

DARREN

APPARENTLY, MY BODY DECIDED I'D OVERDONE it because when I woke up, the bed beside me was empty. I rolled over, still half-asleep to feel the cool sheets beneath my fingers but no sign of Edith. I sat up and looked around, noting the door was partially open. Before I could get out of bed, Edith appeared carrying a tray with breakfast and coffee.

"You're awake," She said with a smile.

I rubbed my face. "How long was I out?"

"Sixteen hours," she answered cheerily.

"Fuck," I groaned and flopped down against the pillow.

She set the tray down and crawled into bed beside me. "You pushed yourself too quickly and your body needed the time to recover and rest. You will be no good to anyone, least of all your allies, if you aren't strong enough to even stand on your own two feet," she said, stroking my cheek.

I craned my neck towards the tray. "What did you bring?"

She laughed. "Are you really interested in food right now?"

I looked back at her. "Gotta keep my strength up."

She kissed my cheek and in the split second it took for me to process the feeling of her lips against my skin, she'd brought back the tray piled high with bacon, eggs, and hash browns.

"Did you make this?"

"You don't have to sound so skeptical. I was raised by a very traditional mother who believed a woman ought to know how to cook."

I held up my hands to placate her. "I'm not criticizing, I just … didn't know you could cook that's all." Before I could say anything else that came across as insulting, I shoveled the food into my mouth, barely taking time to savor how perfectly seasoned the hash browns were, or the expert fluffiness of the eggs. Within minutes I pushed the tray away, my belly full, and the plate empty.

"Feel better?" She moved the tray to the floor.

I wrapped my arms around her waist and pulled her down on top of me, kissing her hard on the mouth. When I finally pulled away, I replied, "What do you think?"

She pressed her hands to my chest, fingers splayed. "Promise me that this will not be the last time we do this."

"I will do everything I can to make sure," I replied, before bucking my hips and reversing our positions on the bed.

She let out a girlish giggle as I kissed her neck, my hands moving down her body. They traced the now-familiar curve of her hips and thighs. If we were about to face the biggest fight of our lives, I was going to enjoy every minute of our time together.

I tried to block out every other sound, smell, and sight except for Edith. The way her chest barely rose and fell, the coolness of her skin beneath my body as we shed our clothes. The hint of grease that clung to her from the food she'd made. There was a time all of those things would have turned me off, but not today. Not now. Not with her. I even relished the tips of her fangs protruding from her mouth as she moaned in pleasure beneath me.

Sometime later—time had lost all meaning—we lay together beneath the tangle of sheets, curled up against each other, totally spent. I closed my eyes, letting sleep come for me. If we were lucky, it wouldn't be the last time we slept in each other's arms.

Danny had been too weak to come along, which was the only good thing I could say about this mission. Darkness fell around us as we crouched behind a row of hedges lining the property two houses up from where I'd grown up. It was a vacant plot of land, but even in the pitch black I could make out the manicured lawn, and the tiny cross, marking the losses suffered here. I would not let Heartsong take anything else from me, not here. Every other able-bodied Hunter had loaded up and taken up positions around the block.

"He will show up," Edith said, almost reading my mind.

"Unless he realizes we figured out his twisted plan and decided to change things up."

She shook her head. "He is a calculating man, but he is also stuck in his ways. He has waited this long to reclaim a victory he believes is his. He has had us on the defensive for months and he will not lose that advantage."

Across the street, a light flipped on in the living room. *Damn it. We should have evacuated the block of civilians.* Heartsong and his lackeys would have no qualms about ripping apart people who got in their way. I tapped the com in my ear.

"Harrison, we need to do what we can to get the civilians out of here. We need to reduce the number of targets we've given him."

"We'll go," Caden said, gesturing to himself and the girls.

I waited a beat before I nodded my go ahead. Even if Harrison didn't approve, I would not let innocents get slaughtered. "Tell them to get below ground if possible."

Caden gave me a quick salute before scurrying out of sight. I'd say the girls were right behind him, but they took off like a shot in opposite directions. I leaned against the bushes, starting to worry that Harrison hadn't responded to my hail. I closed my eyes, trying to focus on everything with my other senses. I pressed my fingers to the grass and tried to feel any tiny changes in the ground. The passing of speedy footsteps, the thud of a body hitting the pavement.

"He should have responded by now," Edith murmured, breaking my concentration.

I tapped the com again, switching to the channel Danny was supposed to be monitoring. "Danny, you there?"

"Yeah." He sounded tired but alert. Medical had cleared him to at least sit behind a desk.

"We need a location and status on Harrison and his team."

"Give me a minute." I could hear the tapping of keys over the connection. "He should be about twenty meters off to your left."

"What's his status? I radioed him about clearing civilians, but got no response."

Before Danny could respond, I felt it. The rush of bodies coming at us like a Mack truck. I caught the horde of vampires spilling into the streets from every direction. I took Edith's hand and squeezed it tight. "Are you ready for this?"

"No, but we don't have a choice," she replied.

Together, we leapt over the hedgerow, weapons in hand. It took all of five seconds for me to lose her in the fray. I could see flashes of metal around me as other Hunters wielded their blades and pens. I heard a snarl from my right and turned, flinging a pen at the oncoming vamp. The pen landed solidly in its chest, dropping it like a stone.

One down.

I bent long enough to pull the pen free and wiped the trail of blue blood on his shirt before moving on. The press of bodies soon became like some bizarre dance as I dodged blows, slammed my fist into as many throats as I could, and lost a pen or two embedded too deep in someone's chest cavity.

The adrenaline coursing through my veins was almost electric as I moved. Like I'd taken the taser energy they'd hit me with and turned it to my own advantage. The numbness and weakness that had still plagued me seemed a distant memory.

"Behind you!" Caden's voice rang out.

I skidded to a halt and turned. Before I could make it all the way around, a blur sped past me, materializing as Edith, as she pinned down a vampire, slamming a pen into his chest. Her hands came away stained blue. I'd never been more in love with someone in my life.

"I'm going to find Harrison," I yelled above the carnage.

She nodded before taking off in another direction. I started advancing on Harrison's last known position, the fighting seeming to move out of my way as I progressed. I was within two feet of where he should be when I collided with something heavy.

I landed on the ground, a heavy body pressing down on me. I clawed at them, my hands coming away covered in red. *Human blood*. Taking a slow breath to bring my adrenaline-fueled reflexes under control, I rolled the body off of me. It landed beside me with a meaty thump. I rolled to one side and pushed myself to my knees. Peering down at the figure, my stomach lurched.

"Darren, can you hear me?" Danny's voice crackled in my ear. The collision must have jarred my com.

"I'm here," I answered.

"The system says Harrison should be right on top of you."

He did not understand just how right he was. The man who'd rescued me, who'd given me purpose and beat my ass into becoming the soldier he needed, lay on the ground, his throat gone. His eyes were glassy and unfixed. For all of his training, he hadn't seen his attacker coming. Had it been Heartsong himself or one of his cronies?

"Darren?" Danny's voice filled my ear.

"Harrison is dead," I reported.

"What?"

"You heard me."

"Damn," Danny breathed.

I had no other words for what I was witnessing. I pressed Harrison's eyelids closed and did my best to drag him out of the line of fire. If we survived this shit show, he deserved a proper burial.

"Oh … shit!" Danny's tone jarred me from the numbness. "What happened?"

"They're here. They found us."

The comm link went dead.

Mother-fucking vampires.

In the dark, it was difficult to pick out friend from foe, but I knew the face I was searching for. I couldn't find him. Not with my limited human senses. I was primed to step forward and go looking when someone grabbed my hand. I whirled, pen poised to find Hope clutching my hand.

"We got them all to safety," she said. Her eyes were wide, and she pressed closer to me as she took in everything around us. Her gaze drifted down to Harrison, and she gave a little yelp.

She was losing her nerve and that was going to get one of us killed. “Listen to me, you can’t lose your shit right now. Not when I need you.”

Her cool fingers slid out of my grasp. “What do you mean?”

“I need to find Heartsong. I know he’s here. But you’ve got better night vision than me.”

She straightened her shoulders. “I can do that.” She turned up the street away from where my family home used to be. I could make out her brow furrowing as she concen-trated. She’d spent so much time trying to act human, she’d let her vampire senses dull. Even with the training we’d pushed on them, they were still just kids. Her head turned back towards me and her hand shot out in front of her. “There. Across the street.”

I followed her hand and spotted his gaunt, smug face among the bodies clashing. He stood there looking bored. Our gazes met, and he gave me a wicked smile before he kicked some-thing.

“What did he just kick?” I ground out.

“Um, a little cross.”

That bastard was on *my* land. He was going to regret every bad decision he ever made bringing him to this very moment. I started across the street, shoving bodies out of the way as I went.

“You can’t face him by yourself,” Hope called, skidding to a halt and pressing her hands to my chest. “Mama E would never forgive me if something happened to you.”

“Kid, I’m doing this for her. For all of us. I’m putting an end to this madness. Now, get out of my way.”

"No. I won't let you face him by yourself."

"No offense, but you pose little threat to him," I argued, hating myself for taking the time in the middle of the fucking battle to argue with a teenager.

"We're stronger together." The look of sheer determination in her eyes melted a little of my annoyance.

I didn't have time to agree to her statement before she lurched forward, blue blood staining the front of her shirt. It dribbled out of her mouth as she fell forward. I scanned the area, looking to see where the blade protruding from her had come from. Heartsong stood there dusting off his hands, and I realized it was the same blade he'd used to kill Ronan months ago in the park.

"Hang in there, Hope. You're going to be fine," I told her as I pulled her out of the line of fire.

"Mama," she burbled.

I looked up in time to see the expression of horror on Edith's face.

CHAPTER TWENTY-FIVE

EDITH

I HAD NEVER RUN AS FAST IN MY ENTIRE LIFE OR afterlife than I did at that moment, to reach Hope in time. In time for what? I was not sure, but I knew she needed me, and I … I needed her.

"What happened? Who did this?" I asked Darren as I sunk to my knees in front of Hope and gathered her into my lap. Instinct told me to pull out whatever impaled her, but what medical training I had through the Red Cross told me to leave it. Pulling out whatever was stopping the bleeding would make it worse. She'd bleed out before we'd have time to fix her.

"Who do you think?" Darren nodded towards his family's property. I caught a flash of Heartsong moving off to the back of the action like a general, watching others fight the fight for him. He never wanted to get his own hands bloody, yet, in this instance, he did. He inflicted more pain with one throw of a knife than a hundred vampire soldiers killing a hundred Hunters could. He wanted me to suffer and suffer I would.

"Mama," Hope whimpered. She blinked several times as if to make sure I was really there before holding out her hand. I clasped it tight.

"I'm here, *Bopha*. I'm here."

"Twenty-five, twenty-six, twenty-seven, twenty-eight ..." I heard Darren counting under his breath as he provided cover.

"Are you honestly keeping a kill tally right now?" I snapped.

"Hey, the world doesn't stop because one soldier gets hurt," he said.

"She is not one soldier! She is a child, and he hurt her! Now, tell me what to do to fix her!" My voice rose to hysterics. I knew I should be calm—I could think better when I was calm—but my mind and emotions refused to listen. This was my baby. My sweet little Hope. How could I be powerless to help her? Mothers always helped. How could I not know what to do when she needed me most?

Darren executed three leg sweeps on the nearest vampires before staking each. "We've spent so much time fixing up our own, we never thought to figure out how to fix a vampire. I'm not sure there's much we *can* do, Edith."

"But she's my world," I whispered, stroking Hope's hair back from her pale, wide-eyed face with my free hand. "She and Angel both have been my entire world for nearly fifty years. There must be something we can do."

"Make her comfortable," Darren suggested. "Stay with her. I'll provide you as much cover as I can. I can't fix her, but I can give you time. As much time as you need to say goodbye."

I nodded, the inevitable beginning to sink in. "Can you find Angel for me?"

Darren shook his head. "No time." He threw a small knife at someone behind us, dropping a vampire before he could harm us. "We can move her away from the fight, but that's the best any of us can do right now. Try not to jostle the knife. It will only make it quicker and more painful."

I cradled Hope against my chest, heading for the relative safety of the sidewalk in a half-crouch. Once there, I sunk to the ground and settled Hope's head in my lap, all the way, being very careful not to touch the knife.

"Mama, It's okay. I'm not afraid to die." Blue blood dribbled out of Hope's mouth with each word. She smiled, her eyes unnaturally bright. I had seen enough death in my long time on Earth to know it would not be long now. "Angel used to say we walked with death every day back in Cambodia. I wasn't afraid then, and I'm not afraid now. You found us and brought us life, Mama. It's been a good life. I promise. You gave us a good life." She squeezed my hand, though not as strongly as before.

"You and your sister are my life." I smoothed her hair back and kissed her cool forehead. "Thank you for giving me such a good life."

Hope shook her head with effort. "We're not your only family now. You've got Darren and Dan and Caden. Love them too, Mama. Love them for me."

"*Knyohm sralaing ahwn*," I whispered.

Hope smiled, repeating 'I love you' in her native language, before her body went from cool, to clammy, to icy in my arms.

I stayed seated on the cool cement of the sidewalk, watching and waiting for Hope's chest to rise and fall again. When it didn't, I closed her eyes and whispered a Cambodian prayer for the dead near her ear. Her spirit could still hear me. I could feel it.

"Mayday. Mayday," Dan's voice crackled over the silence of the comm link in all of our ears, rousing me from my grief. "Mayday. We are under siege. I repeat. We are under siege. We barricaded ourselves in the medical wing, but I … I don't know how long we can hold them. If you can hear this, send help. I repeat, send help."

"On my way," Parker's voice said into the com from wherever he was in the battle carnage. "Hang on, Dan."

"Take a team and go with him," Darren called to Samantha, who was the closest hunter with any bit of authority. "And report back as soon as you know anything."

"Yes, sir." Sam motioned at several team members who all broke away from the fight to return to base.

"As soon as you know anything!" Darren yelled again as they disappeared. He swiveled towards me. "Edith? How you doing?"

"Hope is free from pain," I said. "She is at eternal rest now."

Pain flashed across Darren's face. Not because he himself was hurting, but because I was. Darren Paxton feeling empathy for a vampire?

"We'll get that bastard Heartsong, Edith," he vowed. "I swear to you, he's dust. For everything he's done to our families, he's dust."

"I know he is," I said. "There is no other way for him to leave here today."

I slid Hope off my lap and arranged her arms over her chest. Besides the knife I still couldn't bear to remove from her back, she looked as if she was merely sleeping. I wished to think of her in those terms. *She was merely sleeping.* I leaned close to kiss her forehead before I wiped my blue-stained hands against my skirt and stood up. Mr. Heartsong had disappeared to the back of the Paxton property near a grove of four oak trees. I remembered planting the trees myself twelve years ago. One for each life, I thought, lost in the fire. I caught a flash of Mr. Heartsong's tattered jacket sleeve among the trees. He was still there. Waiting.

"He's there," I said to Darren, and motioned towards the trees. He nodded understanding and followed me in that direction.

Mr. Heartsong stepped out in the open before we reached him, his smile smug as usual and his expression appearing bored at all the death and destruction raging around us. The death and destruction he ordered. "I appear to have misplaced my knife somewhere, Edith my dear. Have you found it?"

I clenched my hands into fists, unwilling to give him the satisfaction of seeing my tears. He could have my anger, but not my tears. "It's over, Percival. You've lost."

He cocked his head to the side at my use of his Christian name. "Lost? Oh, no, I have only just begun. Once I right the wrongs to vampire kind, that the pathetic humans dealt us all those years ago, they will see what it is like to be subjugated. They will live under my rule. My laws. Not the other way around. We will never live by their rules again."

"You cannot force an entire species to bend to your will," I said.

"And why not? They did it to us. They forgot one thing, though. They forgot we are better, stronger, and faster. We are superior to humans in every way. My one regret is that it took so long to put my plan in motion." Mr. Heartsong shrugged. "No matter, though. I would wait forever for my revenge."

"But we *are* human," I countered. "Or were once. Have you forgotten what it was like to be alive? To be one of them?"

"Why would I want to remember?" he sneered. "In all my long years, I have never belonged to one tribe. I have always been between worlds. Navajo. White-Man. Vampire. Human. I discovered quite early on, if I wanted to belong, I needed to create my own tribe. My own clan. So I did."

"You mean your God damned cult?" Darren asked. I caught the flash of light on metal as he slid two blades from his jacket sleeves into his palms, ready for a fight. "Give it up, old man. You're not a ruler. You're a failure. You lost this war once. You're gonna lose it again."

"Do you recognize where we are at, Mr. Paxton?" Mr. Heartsong scuffed the ground with the toe of his worn boot. "This is the very spot I lit the match that killed your parents. You'll be happy to know they died a slow, painful death. Even now, I can still hear their voices, calling for you and your brother. I planned to snuff you all out that night. That is one more mistake I aim to correct today. This time, though, it will be your brother's voice that you hear crying out your name as you stand powerless to stop his fate. Just as you were powerless to stop your parents'. Go ahead. Call him on your communication link. See if he responds."

"Go to hell, you sick fuck." Darren lobbed one of his blades. Mr. Heartsong deflected it as if he was swatting a fly, reacting as if having weapons thrown at him was more of a nuisance than anything to fear.

"Tsk, tsk. Watch your language. There is a lady present."

"I don't care," Darren howled. "You die today, old man."

"No, Mr. Paxton." Mr. Heartsong's eyes glinted in the dim dawn light. "*You* die today." He grinned, enjoying his sadistic game of cat and mouse. "There will always be a place for you in the clan, Edith my dear. And in my bed."

"Never." I clutched my weapon tighter. "I will never return to the clan. This ends now."

Mr. Heartsong shrugged as if to say "as you wish", the same bored expression on his face as when Darren threw the pocketknife at him. He smiled again, fangs flashing, before stepping towards us … only to be pulled back against the tree when a knife came out of nowhere, embedded in his chest, and pinned him to the tree. It missed the mark of his heart, but this attack did not mean to kill him. It was meant to make him suffer. In a flash, I recognized the blade. It was the same that killed Ronan and Hope. Darren and I turned to see Angel standing behind us, hand still up in a throwing stance.

"No one hurts my sister and gets away with it," she told her grand-sire. "Not even you." Angel dusted her hands off just like Mr. Heartsong had done. "Oh, and Darren? Dan's alive. Parker checked in on the com. The barricade held. He and everyone else in the medical wing are fine."

"For now," Mr. Heartsong taunted.

Darren flung his second blade at Mr. Heartsong, pinning his other shoulder to the tree. He produced a wooden stake from his back pocket next and held it out to me. "Do you want to do the honors or should I?"

I closed his fingers around the stake and covered his hand with mine. "Not apart. Together. We do this together."

He nodded. "On three?"

We counted down, and together we drove the death blow into Mr. Heartsong's chest. His eyes widened and his mouth opened in silent death screams before he turned to nothing but dust.

The death screams also released the vampire cult army from whatever glamour Mr. Heartsong had over them all. With their leader gone, their only loyalty was to themselves.

"Where are we?" a recruit asked as the glamour broke. He looked around him, expression puckered in confusion.

"Surrender!" the senior most Hunter official left standing called out.

"Or else what?" another vampire asked.

"Or else death," the official promised. "We can keep fighting until you are all dust, or you can surrender, and we figure out where we go from here … together."

"There doesn't have to be endless distrust between humans and vampires," I called to the crowd. "We can work together. We can live together in peace too, if both sides agree to try."

The vampire cult looked around at each other and everyone laid down their weapons. I reached down to clasp Darren's hand. It seemed they wished to stop fighting and live instead of die at the hands of the Hunters. It was a smart choice. It was the right choice.

Darren eyed the scene, the last vestige of his 'the only good vampire is a dead vampire' creed, dying with the clan's wish for peace.

Long ago, I worked with the Vampire-Human Alliance for equal rights. It was the same fight Angel, Dan, and their friends struggled with now. You could not truly make a difference unless both sides worked together. Was this that moment? Were we truly at a crossroads in vampire-human relations?

"Let's go home," Darren murmured against my hair. "I need to see Danny with my own eyes to make sure the kid is okay."

I nodded wordlessly and leaned against him. The adrenaline of the day drained from me in a rush, leaving nothing but sadness.

"Mama E?" Angel stepped forward, eyes searching mine, as if she was afraid I would admonish her for throwing a knife at her grand-sire, no matter how twisted of a monster he had become. "I had to do it, Mama E. I had to do it for Hope."

"I know, *Bopha*," I whispered, holding out an arm for her. "I know. Let's go home."

The rest of the day passed in a blur. We were reunited with our loved ones back at the base and planned for the burial of our fallen. Angel alternated between clinging to mine or Caden's side, numb with grief for the younger sister she had always protected, and a little lost on what to do without her. We both felt that way. What would we do now without her?

"Have you ever thought of rejoining the VHA?" Caden asked that night as we lingered in the hallway outside Angel's room, waiting for her to fall asleep. "If the governments are really going to make a go of working together for the betterment of human-vampire relations, we could use all the help we can get."

I shook my head. "That means going to Washington. I can't leave Angel. Not now."

"Take her with," Caden said. "It's what Angel and I talked about doing anyway after graduation. This entire war and what happened to Hope just kind of sped that timeline up is all. Me, Dan, Parker, Hope, Angel ... We all planned to fight the good fight and all that." He ran a hand through his hair, expression sheepish. "You're like the most diplomatic person I know. We could really use you in our corner."

"Thank you for the vote of confidence," I murmured. "I appreciate it."

We waited in silence in the hallway until we were positive Angel was asleep, before Caden moved off to his room and I made my way back to ours. Darren was still awake, lying in bed, staring at the ceiling.

"How's Angel?" he asked when I shut the door softly behind me.

"Asleep," I sighed. I undressed almost mechanically and changed into my nightgown. "Caden asked me to rejoin the

Vampire-Human Alliance, and travel with them to Washington, to help with any new treaties and rules that come from this tentative peace," I said. "He thinks I can do a lot of good. Perhaps more than I did in the past."

"What did you say?" Darren asked, voice flat.

"I did not say anything." I pulled back the covers and crawled into my side of the bed. "That is not a decision I plan to make alone. Your opinion matters, Darren. I wouldn't want to do something you disapprove of."

"Why would I shit all over the VHA?" he asked, not looking at me. "Danny is in the VHA."

"If I say yes, I don't know how long I would be gone for," I said. "It could be a week, a month, a year. There is no time frame for rebuilding vampire-human relations."

"So what?" he asked. "You want me to wait?"

"We both know patience is not your strong suit." I curled up against him, feeling the warmth of his body against the coolness of mine. "I would understand if you did not want to wait. I would understand if you did not want me anymore. You did not sign up for a part-time girlfriend."

"I signed up for you and everything you bring." Darren shifted to wrap his arms around me and pulled me tighter against him. He rested his chin against the top of my head. "If that means waiting a week, month, or year, I'll do it."

"Thank you," I murmured. "I don't deserve you."

"Yeah, I'm a real fucking saint," he joked, before kissing the top of my head. "Just come back, okay?"

"I will," I promised. I lay in his arms, letting the steady sound of his heartbeat lull me into a sense of peace. I had wanted to be part of the Paxton family for so long, it still felt slightly unreal to know that now I was. I may have wanted to be Daniel's wife, but perhaps I was fated to be Darren's girlfriend. So many circumstances and moments needed to align in order for us to meet during the recruitment weekend. Perhaps this was exactly where I was meant to be and who I was meant to be with. I reached back to undo the clasp of my locket with Daniel's pictures inside and placed it atop the dresser. Daniel was my past. Darren was my present and my future.

EPILOGUE

DARREN

1 YEAR LATER

THE WHIR OF THE DRILL FILLED MY EARS AS I leaned forward, glaring at the wall bracket that had been the bane of my existence for the last twenty minutes. It shouldn't be this damn hard to mount a shelf. Voices carried from down the hall and I set the drill aside, following the laughter to the kitchen. Danny stood by the fridge, Parker beside him.

"I thought you were supposed to be double checking everything is setup upstairs," I snapped.

Some things will never change. Danny pivoted and stood at attention at the sound of my voice. Parker was slower to react despite his heightened senses, and he too eventually turned to look at me.

"It's ready. You're the one that's taking an eternity to put up a shelf," he jabbed. "And I was just showing Parker the um ... reject cake."

I rushed forward and pushed them both out of the way, eyeing the sad attempt at baking I'd engaged in. I'd never been accused of being a wonderful cook, but today was too important for my pathetic skills to ruin things. "I told you to throw it away."

Danny snickered. "You know she won't let you off the hook for it."

"It shows how much you care," Parker added.

I reached into the fridge and grabbed a beer before heading back to the living room. I heard footsteps on the hardwood flooring and Danny appeared. "You know it's a bad idea to drink and operate power tools."

I flashed him a smile and pointed from him to the drill. "Did I say anything about operating a power tool while drinking?"

"You're such a dick," he muttered, but picked up the drill and got the bracket secured by the time I'd finished my beer.

"She's going to like it, right?" I said, as I clapped my brother on the back and studied the photographs Parker had brought in and tastefully arranged.

"She's going to love it," Danny answered.

Out of the corner of my eye, I noticed Parker fiddling with his phone. "Angel says they're ten minutes out. I'm going to wait for them outside."

I waited for him to leave before I turned to my brother. "When did he get to be so insightful?"

Danny snorted. "He's into psych stuff, remember? I think since everything has finally settled down, he feels like he can be himself and he's happy with who that is."

"And you're happy together?"

"Yes, Darren. I am happy with my boyfriend."

"Even though he's like eighty?"

Danny sighed. "I look at him and I see the hot guy who caught my eye. I don't see someone old. Sure, he's got way more experience than me, but that's not a bad thing. The longer we're together, the more I can learn from his experience."

"Good."

He wrapped the cord around the drill and set it back in the toolkit. "It still feels kind of weird being here. Not that the house looks anything like it used to, but … with everything that has happened here, you know?"

"Yeah. I know what you mean. But this is home. And that's important to remember."

"He's right, you know. She's going to love this," he added.

"They're here!" Parker's voice echoed from the front hallway.

I grabbed the tool kit and returned it to the cabinet above the sink in the kitchen before I joined Danny and Parker on the front lawn. Thanks to Angel and Caden, flowers surrounded the little grave marker I'd made. I hadn't been sure how it would look, but they'd done a good job and it felt like it honored everything that had been sacrificed here.

A car pulled into the driveway. I spotted Edith in the backseat once Angel and Caden got out of the car. Caden rounded the back of the vehicle while Angel opened the back door and helped Edith out of the car, a blindfold obscuring her vision. I had my doubts whether she really couldn't see through some flimsy fabric, but she was playing along.

"Would you two please tell me what is going on?" she demanded.

I stopped up to her, wrapped my arms around her waist and kissed her, leaving the blindfold on. I expected her to tense, but she melted into me. She'd been gone too long.

"Can I please take this thing off now?" she whispered.

"Only if you're ready for a surprise," I answered, and stepped to the side so I wouldn't obstruct her view.

She pulled her blindfold free and stared up at the house. She turned, spotted the grave marker, and then looked back at me. "Did you … is this what you've been doing all year?"

I grinned. "While you've been championing for human and vampire equality, I've been building us a home."

"It's beautiful."

"Wait until you see the inside."

I grabbed her hand and tugged her along inside, leading her straight down the hallway to the living room. She stopped short, eying the photographs on the mantle. Memories of both of our pasts.

"Thank you."

"I'll show you the bedroom when the kids are gone," I said with a wink.

She chuckled and reached up to stroke my cheek. She patted my face and tilted her head to one side. "Why are they arguing about a reject?"

Sometimes, I still wasn't used to her superhuman hearing. "Uh, well, a year ago, in that diner, I told you that this year, you were turning twenty-three. And I intend to keep that promise."

I led her through the small dining room and into the kitchen where Danny had thankfully laid out the store-bought birthday cake I'd gotten.

"That doesn't look like a reject," she said.

Danny and his friends devolved into gales of laughter as he pointed to the painful attempt I'd made. Color warmed the nape of my neck. "I tried, but I'm better with power tools than baking."

She gave it a suspicious look before wrapping her arms around my neck. "It is the thought that counts. Thank you. This is wonderful."

Parker brought out plates and utensils, and Caden started carving up the cake. Edith and I stepped back and watched our little family. So much pain and loss had defined us all for such a long time. Maybe now we could finally find some peace.

"I have been thinking," Edith murmured, as she leaned into my chest.

"Yeah?"

"As strange as it sounds, I think fate ensured these series of events so you and I could find each other when the time was right. If you had not walked into my life that weekend, I don't know what would have happened or where we would be now."

I considered her words for a long moment. "I've never been one for fate, but I can't deny that my life is better with you in it. Maybe you're right and everything happened for a reason. Whatever comes next, I want you to know that we're going to face it together."

THE END.

MORE READS

CayellePublishing.com

amazon.com

CayéllePublishing.com